The Writings of Owen Wister

MEMBERS OF THE FAMILY

The Writings of Owen Wister

RED MEN AND WHITE

LIN McLEAN

HANK'S WOMAN

THE VIRGINIAN

MEMBERS OF THE FAMILY

WHEN WEST WAS WEST

LADY BALTIMORE

SAFE IN THE ARMS OF CROESUS

U. S. GRANT AND THE SEVEN AGES
OF WASHINGTON

THE PENTECOST OF CALAMITY AND
THE STRAIGHT DEAL

NEIGHBORS HENCEFORTH

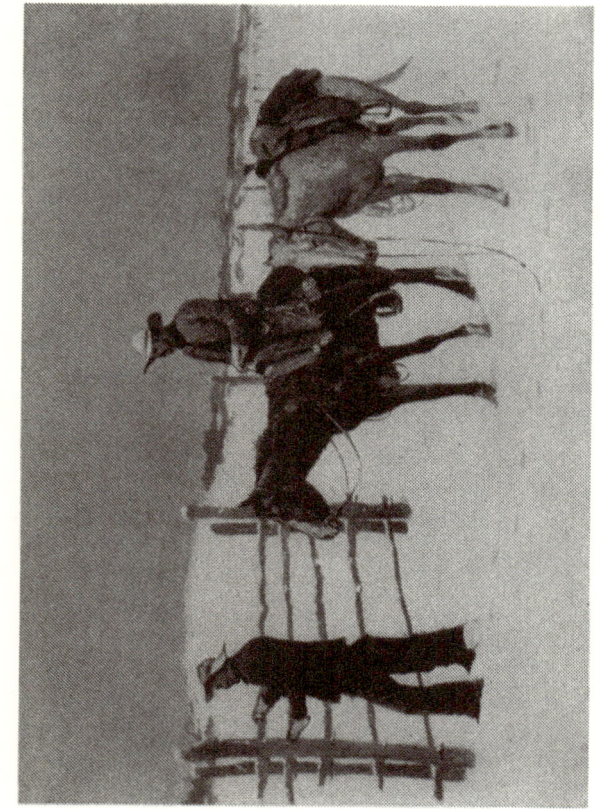

THE FALL OF THE COWBOY

From a painting by Frederic Remington

The Writings of Owen Wister

of The American Academy of Arts and Letters

Membre Correspondant de la Société
des Gens de Lettres

Honorary Fellow of the Royal Society of Literature

Members of the Family

PRINTED IN THE UNITED STATES OF AMERICA BY
R. R. DONNELLEY & SONS CO., AT THE LAKESIDE PRESS, CHICAGO

TO

HORACE HOWARD FURNESS

OF LINDENSHADE, WALLINGFORD

That is my home of love: if I have rang'd,
Like him that travels, I return again.
—SONNET CIX.

. . . *mihi parva rura et*
Spiritum Graiae tenuem Camenae
Parca non mendax dedit, et malignum
Spernere vulgus.

PREFACE—*"Thanking You in Advance"*

THE first tale in this collection was written in 1900, the last in 1910, and the volume appeared in April, 1911. Its reviewer in the *New York Evening Post* pronounced it to be merely scraps and parings, left over from *The Virginian*. This same critic discovered in the final story, which concerns the conjugal strategy of some ducks in a pond, and its happy effect upon their youthful owner, an unsuccessful attempt to repeat the story of Em'ly, who was a hen. Pray observe the suspicious circumstance of twice introducing domestic fowls into fiction.

The Golden Book has, during the last few years, republished pretty much all these scraps and parings.

In *Babel*, among the letters written by readers of the duck story to its highly gratified author, is a particularly delightful one, which suggests: Why not add a third lady to the group in Jimsy's pond, and see what they would all do then?

Could I have returned to the ranch on that river in Wyoming, where, week after week in

1910, I watched and recorded the behavior of Sir Francis and his two wives as they swam in their pond, what developments would have been precipitated? Without trying to experiment, I could predict the deplorable consequences to a certainty; but so can any man— provided that he has had in his life some intimations of the primitive instincts of woman.

Everything of mine published subsequently to this volume must be regarded as posthumous, if the newspapers are to be credited. According to them, I died on October 13, 1911. But more than that, I am reported to have died not only at Cleveland, Ohio, but also in Wyoming, on the same day. Very few persons have been able to die so widely. Moreover, the news was run off on the ticker in the New York stock exchange, which is surely the nearest you can come in America to being buried in Westminster Abbey. I never weary of reading my obituaries.

As I look over the volume of *Babel* wherein these are pasted, there's but one word to say to our newspapers: "Thanking you in advance."

"Thanking you in advance" is a phrase which terminates multitudes of letters that come to me—as they must to thousands of fellow-sufferers—every year. These all cheerfully and confidently ask you to make a free gift to them of your time, attention, and energy. A girl of fifteen or a student at High School, wants your autograph, or your photograph, or the story of your life to put in a composition they are writing, or all of these at once; and some of them beg you to be quick about it. A lady asks for a sentiment, or your favorite text in the Bible, or your favorite poem; another wishes you to tell her your reasons for writing what you have written; a library, a school, a hospital, asks you for money; a bed-ridden invalid desires an autographed copy of one of your works—and nearly all of them "thank you in advance." Do they imagine that this is good manners?

I wonder if my fellow-sufferers vary in their temper, like me, and reply to these requests sometimes amiably, unamiably at others, and often not at all? Or am I a sinner among a flock of saints? I wish I had back all the time I have wasted on idle and futile correspondents, and I feel never a twinge of compunction for the answers which I wrote to some of them. As for "thanking in advance"—when I see those cheap, stereotyped words now-a-days—that settles it! the waste-basket instantly receives the communication.

Babel is a treasure-house of opinions: I find

a letter telling me I'm a corrupter of youth;
another begins, "Infamous novelist"; all in
the same week, the president of Harvard in-
vites me to teach a class in English literature
at that seat of foot-ball; a tobacco company
asks leave to call its new 5-cent cigar *The Virginian,* a newspaper wishes me, in company
with United States senators and other recog-
nized authorities on the subject, to state in not
over 500 words my views upon the immortal-
ity of the soul, and an outraged Presbyterian
divine accuses me of being an Episcopal
propagandist.

From Babel, 1908, I give this specimen, pro-
posing collaboration with the writer... "in an
ambitious novel to be a World-Beater, instead
of 'One of the 5 Best sellers!'—to be entitled
THE WORLD'S MASTER; A Tale of the
Panic of 1907-8, with Rockefeller and Mor-
gan, and Roosevelt, Taft and Bryan in the
cast.

"It is to be based upon the DEMONSTRA-
BLE economic truth that the Gold Dollar, as
the COINAGE standard, or MEASURE, of
our dollar—the CONTRACT dollar, is a CON-
FISCATING standard—causing FOUR BIL-
LION dollars of confiscation in '93, in this
Nation ALONE; through a 25% rise in gold

in the SPRING of '93, due to an increased
demand for GOLD as legal tender, exclusively, of THREE AND ONE HALF billion
dollars in Austro-Hungary and East India,
which, on Rothschild PRESSURE, adopted
the SINGLE gold coinage standard May 20,
'93 and June 26, '93, respectively. ALL other
gold standard Nations suffered the SAME
confiscation (25% added to all private debts,
with UNIVERSAL RUIN, as here); while
Mexico, retaining the SILVER coinage, was
MORE prosperous than ever in her history.
This is a shining object lesson of the truth.

"These facts, elaborated and submitted to
the Monetary Commission in October '97, elic-
ited Chairman Edmunds' letter of thanks,
saying my Paper was 'one of the BRIGHT-
EST and BEST' of the several hundred he
had received from all over the Nation. Secretary L. J. Gage, being called on to REFUTE
my Paper, CONCEDED all its positions: his
ONLY plea for the gold COINAGE standard
being that it had reduced interest from 6% to
3%. The FACT of CONFISCATION of the
GOLD CONTRACT dollar is on a ROCK
foundation. I can satisfy you of that beyond a
question.

"BOILED DOWN to one chapter of about

17 pages, I have the WHOLE engrossing
Story of the rise of the House of Rothschild
to its present MASTERY of the World, in-
cluding its campaign of 25 years, since 1867
to put the World on the SINGLE gold standard, with its JUGGERNAUT of UNTOLD
billions of confiscation; to the culmination: the
ownership of ALL the GOLD of the world, by
owning 50 per cent more of the Government
Gold Bonds than the supply of gold; and its
power to RAISE and DEPRESS gold, AT
ITS WILL, by ARTIFICIAL scarcity; with
ALTERNATE Panic and Prosperity — a
SCOOP NET, such as that Satanic Genius,
Nathan Mayer R. had from 1816 to 1836, by
OWNING the key to the financial stocks of
Europe:

"If we agree, I will send that Chapter, and
a SUGGESTED Outline of a Plot, to you as
a BASIS on which YOU will make the Plot
and distribute the work.

"Your prompt attention will be appreciated...."

I lamented to him my utter unworthiness
for this collaboration, and, feeling particularly frisky that morning, gave him several
names of distinguished confrères, intimating
that any one of them would jump at it; and

waited results. These presently followed.
Dated from Tasmania, Feb. 9, '09, a duplicate
of his request to me arrived, and across the
top of it was scrawled:

"Dear Wister:—Gee! Haven't I troubles
enough of my own? Anyway I've passed him
along. Jack London."

It's not the checks we scribblers receive
for our wares that are our reward—they're
merely our pay, earned with the sweat of our
pens: it's letters from across land and sea,
it's meeting horses in the West named after
our characters, it's the kind of friends—and
the kind of enemies—we make, which are the
minted gold of our reward.

OWEN WISTER.

Long House, Bryn Mawr, 1928.

TABLE OF CONTENTS

MEMBERS
OF THE FAMILY

I

SCIPIO LE MOYNE lay in bed, held together with bandages. His body had need for many bandages. A Bar-Circle-Zee three-year-old had done him violent mischief at the forks of Stinking Water.[1] But for the fence, Scipio might have swung clear of the wild, rearing animal. When they lifted his wrecked frame from the ground one of them had said:—

"A spade's all he'll need now."

Overhearing this with some still unconquered piece of his mind, Scipio made one last remark: "I ain't going to die for years and years."

[1] Lately changed to Shoshone River by act of legislature. While we miss the old name, derived from certain sulphur springs, we agree that like the Indian and the cow-boy it belongs to the past.

Upon this his head had rolled over, and no further statements came from him for—I forget how long. Yet somehow, we all believed that last remark of his.

"Since I've known him," said the Virginian, "I have found him a truthful man."

"Which don't mean," Honey Wiggin put in, "that he can't lie when he ought to."

Judge Henry always sent his hurt cow-punchers to the nearest surgical aid, which in this case was the hospital on the reservation. Here then, one afternoon, Scipio lay, his body still bound tight at a number of places, but his brain needing no bandages whatever; he was able to see one friend for a little while each day. It was almost time for this day's visitor to go, and the visitor looked at his watch.

"Oh, don't do that!" pleaded the man in bed. "I'm not sick any more."

"You will be sick some more if you keep talking," replied the Virginian.

"Thinkin' is a heap more dangerous, if y'u can't let it out," Scipio urged. "I'm not half through tellin' y'u about Horacles."

"Did his mother name him that?" inquired the Virginian.

"Naw! but his mother brought it on him. Didn't y'u know? Of course you don't often

get so far north in the Basin as the Agency.
His name is Horace Pericles Byram. Well, the
Agent wasn't going to call his assistant store-
clerk all that, y'u know, not even if he *has* got
an uncle in the Senate of the United States.
Couldn't spare the time. Days not long
enough. Not even in June. So everybody calls
him Horacles now. He's reconciled to it. But
I ain't. It's too good for him. A heap too
good. I've knowed him all my life, and I can't
think of a name that's not less foolish than he
is. Well, where was I? I was tellin y'u how
back in Gallipol*eece* he couldn't understand
anything. Not dogs. Not horses. Not girls.''

"Do you understand girls?" the Virginian
interrupted.

"Better'n Horacles. Well, now it seems he
can't understand Indians. Here he is sellin'
goods to 'em across the counter at the Agency
store. I could sell twiced what he does, from
what they tell me. I guess the agent has begun
to discover what a trick Uncle played him
when he unloaded Horacles on him. Now why
did the Uncle do that?''

Scipio stopped in his rambling discourse,
and his brows knitted as he began to think
about the Uncle. The Virginian once again
looked at his watch, but Scipio, deep in his

thoughts, did not notice him. "Uncle," he resumed to himself, half aloud, "Uncle was the damnedest scoundrel in Gallipol*eece.* — Say!" he exclaimed suddenly, and made an eager movement to sit up. "Oh Lord!" he groaned, sinking back. "I forgot. — What's your hurry?"

But the Virginian had seen the pain transfix his friend's face, and though that face had instantly smiled, it was white. He stood up. "I'd ought to get kicked from here to the ranch," he said, remorsefully. "I'll get the doctor."

Vainly the man in bed protested; his visitor was already at the door.

"I've not told y'u about his false teeth!" shrieked Scipio, hoping this would detain him. "And he does tricks with a rabbit and a bowl of fish."

But the guest was gone. In his place presently the Post surgeon came, and was not pleased. Indeed, this excellent army doctor swore. Still, it was not the first time that he had done so, nor did it prove the last; and Scipio, it soon appeared, had given himself no hurt. But in answer to a severe threat, he whined: —

"Oh, ain't you goin' to let me see him tomorro'?"

"You'll see nobody to-morrow except me."

"Well, that'll be seein' nobody," whined Scipio, more grievously.

The doctor grinned. "In some ways you're incurable. Better go to sleep now." And he left him.

Scipio did not go to sleep then, though by morning he had slept ten healthful hours, waking with the Uncle still at the centre of his thoughts. It made him again knit his brows.

"No, you can't see him to-day," said the doctor, in reply to a request.

"But I hadn't finished sayin' something to him," Scipio protested. "And I'm well enough to see my dead grandmother."

"That I'll not forbid," answered the doctor. And he added that the Virginian had gone back to Sunk Creek with some horses.

"Oh, yes," said Scipio. "I'd forgot. Well, he'll be coming through on his way to Billings next week. You been up to the Agency lately? Yesterday? Well, there's going to be something new happen. Agent seem worried or anything?"

"Not that I noticed. Are the Indians going on the war-path?"

"Nothing like that. But why does a senator of the United States put his nephew in that store? Y'u needn't to tell me it's to provide

for him, for it don't provide. I thought I had
it figured out last night, but Horacles don't fit.
I can't make him fit. He don't understand
Injuns. That's my trouble. Now the Uncle
must know Horacles don't understand. But if
he didn't know?'' pursued Scipio, and fell to
thinking.

"Well," said the doctor indulgently, as
he rose, "it's good you can invent these
romances. Keeps you from fretting, shut
up here alone."

"There'd be no romances here," retorted
Scipio. "Uncle is exclusively hard cash."
The doctor departed.

At his visit next morning, he was pleased
with his patient's condition. "Keep on," said
he, "and I'll let you sit up Monday for ten
minutes. Any more romances?"

"Been thinkin' of my past life," said
Scipio.

The doctor laughed long. "Why, how old
are you, anyhow?" he asked at length.

"Oh, there's some lovely years still to come
before I'm thirty. But I've got a whole lot of
past life, all the same." Then he pointed a solemn, oracular finger at the doctor. "What
white man savvys the Injun? Not you. Not
me. And I've drifted around some, too. The

map of the United States has been my home.
Been in Arizona and New Mexico and among
the Siwashes — seen all kinds of Injun — but
I don't savvy 'em. I know most any Injun's
better'n most any white man till he meets the
white man. Not smarter, y'u know, but better.
And I do know this: You take an Injun and
let him be a warrior and a chief and a grand-
father who has killed heaps of white men in
his day — but all that don't make him grown
up. Not like we're grown up. He stays a child
in some respects till he's dead. He'll believe
things and be scared at things that ain't
nothin' to you and me. You take old High
Bear right on this reservation. He's got hair
like snow and eyes like an eagle's and he can
sing a war-song about fights that happened
when our fathers were kids. But if you want
to deal with him, you got to remember he's a
child of five.''

''I do know all this,'' said the doctor, inter-
ested. ''I've not been twenty years on the
frontier for nothing.''

''Horacles don't know it,'' said Scipio.
''I've saw him in the store all season.''

''Well,'' said the doctor, ''see you to-
morrow. I've some new patients in the ward.''

''Soldiers?''

"Soldiers."

"Guess I know why they're here."

"Oh, yes," sighed the doctor. "You know. Few come here for any other reason." The doctor held views about how the passions of the enlisted man should be acknowledged under supervision, which popular ethics will never permit. "Can I do anything for you?" he inquired.

"If I could have some newspapers?" said Scipio.

"Why didn't you tell me before?" said the doctor. After that he saw to it that Scipio had them liberally.

With newspapers the patient sat surrounded deep, when the Virginian, passing north on his way to Billings, looked in for a moment to give his friend the good word. That is what he came for, but what he said was:—

"So he has got false teeth?"

Scipio, hearing the voice at the door, looked over the top of his paper at the visitor.

"Yes," he replied, precisely as if the visitor had never been out of the room.

"What d' y'u know?" inquired the Virginian.

"Nothing; what do you?"

"Nothing."

After all, such brief greetings cover the ground.

"Better sit down," suggested Scipio.

The Virginian sat, and took up a paper. Thus for a little while they both read in silence.

"Did y'u stop at the Agency as y'u came along?" asked Scipio, not looking up from his paper.

"No."

There was silence again as they continued reading. The Virginian, just come from Sunk Creek, had seen no newspapers as recent as these. When two friends on meeting after absence can sit together for half an hour without a word passing between them, it is proof that they really enjoy each other's company. The gentle air came in the window, bringing the tonic odor of the sage-brush. Outside the window stretched a yellow world to distant golden hills. The talkative voice of a magpie somewhere near at hand was the only sound.

"Nothing in the newspapers in particular," said Scipio, finally.

"You expaictin' something particular?" the Virginian asked.

"Yes."

"Mind sayin' what it is?"

"Wish I knew what it is."

"Always Horacles?"

"Always him — and Uncle. I'd like to spot Uncle."

Mess call sounded from the parade ground. It recalled the flight of time to the Virginian.

"When you get back from Billings," said Scipio, "you're liable to find me up and around."

"Hope so. Maybe you'll be well enough to go with me to the ranch."

But when the Virginian returned, a great deal had happened all at once, as is the custom of events.

Scipio's vigorous convalescence brought him in the next few days to sitting about in the open air, and then enlarged his freedom to a crutch. He hobbled hither and yon, paying visits, many of them to the doctor. The doctor it was, and no newspaper, who gave to Scipio the first grain of that "something particular" which he had been daily seeking and never found. He mentioned a new building that was being put up rather far away down in the corner of the reservation. The rumor in the air was that it had something to do with the Quartermaster's department. The odd thing was that the Quartermaster himself had heard nothing about it. The Agent up at the Agency store considered this extremely odd. But a profound absence of further explanations seemed to prevail. What possible need for a building was there at that inconvenient, isolated spot?

Scipio slapped his leg. "I guess what y'u call my romance is about to start."

"Well," the doctor admitted, "it may be. Curious things are done upon Indian reservations. Our management of them may be likened to putting the Lord's Prayer and the Ten Commandments into a bag and crushing them to powder. Let our statesmen at Washington get their hands on an Indian reservation, and not even honor among thieves remains."

"Say, doc," said Scipio, "when d' y'u guess I can get off?"

"Don't be in too much of a hurry," the doctor cautioned him. "If you go to Sunk Creek—"

"Sunk Creek! I only want to go to the Agency."

"Oh, well, you could do that to-day — but don't you want to see the entertainment? Conjuring tricks are promised."

"I want to see Horacles."

"But he is the entertainment. Supper comes after he's through."

Scipio stayed. He was not repaid, he thought. "A poor show," was his comment as he went to bed.

The next day found him seated in the Agency store, being warmly greeted by his friends the Indians. They knew him well; perhaps he understood them better than he had said. By Horacles he was not warmly greeted; perhaps Horacles did not wish to be understood—and then, Scipio, in his comings and goings through the reservation, had played with Horacles for the benefit of bystanders. There is no doubt whatever that Horacles did not understand Scipio. He was sorry to notice how the Agent, his employer, shook Scipio's hand and invited him to come and stop with him till he was fit to return to his work. And Scipio accepted this invitation. He sat him down in the store, and made himself at home. Legs stretched out on one chair, crutch within reach, hands comfortably clasped round the arms of the chair he sat in, head tilted back, eyes apparently studying the goods which hung from the beams overhead, he visibly sniffed the air.

"Smell anything you don't like?" inquired the clerk, tartly — and unwisely.

"Nothin' except you, Horacles," was the perfectly amiable rejoinder. — "It's good," Scipio then confessed, "to be smellin' buckskin and leather and groceries instead of ether and iodoform."

"Guess you were pretty sick," observed the clerk, with relish.

"Yes. Oh, yes. I was pretty sick. That's right. Yes." Scipio had continued through these slowly drawled remarks to look at the ceiling. Then his glance dropped to the level of Horacles, and keenly fixed that unconscious youth's plump little form, pink little face, and mean little mustache. Behind one ear stuck a pen, behind the other a pencil, as the assistant clerk was arranging some tins of Arbuckle's Arioso coffee. Then Scipio took aim and fired: "So you're going to quit your job?"

Horacles whirled round. "Who says so?"

The chance shot — if there ever is such a thing, if such shots are not always the result of visions and perceptions which lie beyond our present knowledge — this chance shot had hit.

"First I've heard of it," then said Horacles sulkily. "Guess you're delirious still." He returned to his coffee, and life grew more interesting than ever to Scipio.

Instead of trickling back, health began to rush back into his long imprisoned body, and though he could not fully use it yet, and though if he hobbled a hundred yards he was compelled to rest it, his wiry mind knew no fatigue. How athletic his brains were was easily perceived by the Indian Agent. The convalescent would hobble over to the store after breakfast and hail the assistant clerk at once. "Morning, Horacles," he would begin; "how's Uncle?"—"Oh, when are you going to give us a new joke?" the worried Horacles would retort.—"Just as soon as you give us a new Uncle, Horacles. Or any other relation to make us feel proud we know you. What did his letter last night say?" The second or third time this had been asked still found Horacles with no better repartee than angry silence. "Didn't he send me his love?" Scipio then said; and still the hapless Horacles said nothing. "Well, y'u give him mine when you write him this afternoon."—"I ain't writing this afternoon," snapped the clerk.—"You're not! Why I thought you

wrote each other every day!" This was so
near the truth that Horacles flared out: "I'd
be ashamed if I'd nothing better to do than
spy on other people's mails."

Thus by dinner-time generally an audience
would be gathered round Scipio where he sat
with his legs on the chair, and Horacles over
his ledger would be furiously muttering that
"Some day they would all see."

Horacles asked for a couple of days' holiday, and got it. He wished to hunt, he said.
But the Agent happened to find that he had
been to the railroad about some freight. This
he mentioned to Scipio. "I don't know what
he's up to," he said. He had found that
worrying Horacles was merely one of the
things that Scipio's brains were good for;
Scipio had advised him prudently about a sale
of beeves, and had introduced a simple contrivance for luring to the store the customers
whom Horacles failed to attract. It was
merely a free lunch counter,—cheese and
crackers every day, and deviled ham on pay-
day,—but it put up the daily receipts.

And next, one evening after the mail was
in, Scipio, sitting alone in the front of the
store, saw the Agent, sitting alone in the back
of the store, spring suddenly from his chair,

crush a newspaper into his pocket, and stride out to his house. At breakfast the Agent said to Scipio:—

"I must go to Washington. I shall be back before they let you and your leg run loose. Will you do something for me?"

"Name it. Just name it."

"Run the store while I'm gone."

"D' y'u think I can?"

"I know you can. There'll be no trouble under you. You understand Indians."

"But suppose something turns up?"

"I don't think anything will before I'm back. I'd sooner leave you than Horacles in charge here. Will you do it and take two dollars a day?"

"Do it for nothing. Horacles'll be compensation enough."

"No, he won't.—And see here, he can't help being himself."

"Enough said. I'll strive to pity him. None of us was consulted about being born. And I'll keep remembering that we was both raised at Gallipol*eece*, Ohio, and that he inherited a bigger outrage of a name than I did. That's what comes of havin' a French ancestor. —Only, he used to steal my lunch at school." And Scipio's bleached blue eye grew cold.

Later injuries one may forgive, but school ones never.

"Didn't you whale him?" asked the Agent.

"Every time," said Scipio, "till he told Uncle. Uncle was mayor of Gallipole*ece* then. So I wasn't ready to get expelled,—I got ready later; nothin' is easier than gettin' expelled,—but I locked up my lunch after that."

"Uncle's pretty good to him," muttered the Agent. "Got him this position.—Well, nobody will expel you here. Look after things. I'll feel easy to think you're on hand."

For that newspaper which the Agent had crushed into his pocket, Scipio searched cracks and corners, but searched in vain. A fear quite unreasoning possessed him for a while: could he but learn what was in the paper that had so stirred his patron, perhaps he could avert whatever the thing was that he felt in the air, threatening some sort of injury. He knew himself resourceful. Dislike of Horacles and Uncle had been enough to start his wish to thwart them—if there was anything to thwart; but now pride and gratitude fired him; he had been trusted; he cared more to be trusted than for anything on earth; he must rise equal to it now! The Agent had evidently taken the paper away with him—and so Scipio absurdly read all the papers. He collected old ones, and laid his hands upon the new the moment they were out of the mail-bag. It may be said that he lived daily in a wrapping of newspapers.

"Why, you have got Horacles laughing at you." The observant Virginian pointed this out to Scipio immediately on his arrival from Billings. Scipio turned a sickened look upon his friend. The look was accompanied by a cold wave in his stomach.

"Y'u cert'nly have," the remorseless friend pursued. "I reckon he must have had a plumb happy time watchin' y'u still-hunt them newspapers. Now who'd ever have foretold you would afford Horacles enjoyment?"

In a weak voice Scipio essayed to fight it off. "Don't you try to hoodwink me with any of your frog lies."

"No need," said the Virginian. "From the door as I came in I saw him at his desk lookin' at y'u easy-like. 'Twas a right quaint pictyeh —him smilin' at the desk, and your nose tight agaynst the Omaha *Bee*. I thought first y'u didn't have a handkerchief."

"I wonder if he has me beat?" muttered poor Scipio.

The Virginian now had a word of consolation. "Don't y'u see," he again pointed out, "that no newspaper could have helped you? If it could why did he go away to Washington without tellin' you? He don't look for you to deal with troubles he don't mention to you."

"I wonder if Horacles has me beat?" said Scipio once more.

The Virginian standing by the seated, brooding man clapped him twice on the shoulders, gently. It was enough. They were very fast friends.

"I know," said Scipio in response. "Thank y'u. But I'd hate for him to have me beat."

It was the doctor who now furnished information that would have relieved any reasonable man from a sense of failure. The doctor was excited because his view of our faith in Indian matters was again justified by a further instance.

"Oh, yes!" he said. "Just give those people at Washington time, and every step they've taken from the start will be in the mud puddle of a lie. Uncle's in the game all right. He's been meditating how to serve his country and increase his income. There's a railroad at the big end of his notion, but the entering wedge seems only to be a new store down in the corner of this reservation. You see, it has been long settled by the sacredest compacts that two stores shall be enough here—the Post-trader's and the Agent's—but the dear Indians need a third, Uncle says. He has told the Senate and the Interior Department and the White House that a lot of them have to travel too far for supplies. So now Washington is sure the Indians need a third store. The Post-trader and the Agent are stopping at the Post to-night. They got East too late to hold up the job. If Horacles opens that new store, the Agent might just as well shut up his own.''

"Ain't y'u going to look at my leg?" was all the reply that Scipio made.

The doctor laughed. It was to examine the leg that he had come, and he had forgotten all about it. "You can forget all about it, too," he told Scipio when he had finished. "Go back to Sunk Creek when you like. Go back to full work next week, say. Your wicked body is sound again. A better man would unquestionably have died."

But the cheery doctor could not cheer the unreasonable Scipio. In the morning the complacent little Horacles made known to all the world his perfected arrangements. Directly

the Agent had safely turned his back and gone
to Washington, his disloyal clerk had become
doubly busy. He had at once perceived that
this was a comfortable time for him to hurry
his new rival store into readiness and be se-
curely established behind its counter before
his betrayed employer should return. In this
last he might not quite succeed; the Agent
had come back a day or two sooner than
Horacles had calculated, but it was a trifle;
after all, he had carried through the small part
of his uncle's scheme which he had been sent
here to do. Inside that building in the far
corner of the reservation, once rumored to be
connected with the Quartermaster's department, he would now sell luxuries and necessi-
ties to the Indians at a cheaper price than his
employer's, and his employer's store would
henceforth be empty of customers. Perhaps the sweetest moment that Horacles had
known for many weeks was when he said to
Scipio:—

"I'm writing Uncle about it to-day."

That this should have gone on under his
nose while he sat searching the papers was
to Scipio utterly unbearable. His mind was in
a turmoil, feeling about helplessly but furiously for vengeance; and the Virginian's sane

question—What could he have done to stop it if he had discovered it?—comforted him not at all. They were outside the store, sitting under a tree, waiting for the returning Agent to appear. But he did not come, and the suspense added to Scipio's wretchedness.

"He put me in charge," he kept repeating.

"The driver ain't responsible when a stage is held up," reasoned the Virginian.

Scipio hardly heard him. "He put me in charge," he said. Then he worked round to Horacles again. "He ain't got strength. He ain't got beauty. He ain't got riches. He ain't got brains. He's just got sense enough for parlor conjuring tricks—not good ones, either. And yet he has me beat."

"He's got an uncle in the Senate," said the Virginian.

The disconsolate Scipio took a pull at his cigar,—he had taken one between every sentence. "Damn his false teeth."

The Virginian looked grave. "Don't be hasty. Maybe the day will come when you and me'll need 'em to chew our tenderloin."

"We'll be old. Horacles is twenty-five."

"Twenty-five is certainly young to commence eatin' by machinery," admitted the Virginian.

"And he's proud of 'em," whined Scipio.
"Proud! Opens his bone box and sticks 'em
out at y'u on the end of his tongue."

"I hate an immodest man," said the Virginian.

"Why, he hadn't any better sense than to
do it over to the officers' club right before the
ladies and everybody the other night. The
K. O.'s wife said it gave her the creeps—and
she don't look sensitive."

"Well," said the Virginian, "if I weighed
three hundred pounds I'd be turrable sensitive."

"She had to leave," pursued Scipio. "Had
to take her little girl away from the show.
Them teeth comin' out of Horacles'es mouth
the way they did sent the child into hysterics. Y'u could hear her screechin' half
way down the line."

The Virginian looked at his watch. "I wonder if that Agent is coming here at all to-
day?"

Scipio's worried face darkened again.
"What can I do? What *can* I?" he demanded.
And he rose and limped up and down where
the ponies were tied in front of the store. The
fickle Indians would soon be tying these
ponies in front of the rival store. "I received

this business in good shape," continued Scipio, "and I'll hand it back in bad."

Horacles looked out of the door. He wore his hat tilted to make him look like the dare-devil that he was not; dare-devils seldom have soft pink hands, red eyelids, and a fluffy mustache. He smiled at Scipio, and Scipio smiled at him, sweetly and dangerously.

"Would you mind keeping store while I'm off?" inquired Horacles.

"Sure not!" cried Scipio, with heartiness. "Goin' to have your grand opening this afternoon?"

"Well, I *was*," Horacles replied, enjoying himself every moment. "But Mr. Forsythe" (this was the Agent) "can't get over from the Post in time to be present this afternoon. It's very kind of him to want to be present when I start my new enterprise, and I appreciate it, boys, I can tell you. So I sent him word I wouldn't think of opening without him, and it's to be to-morrow morning."

While Horacles was speaking thus, the Indians had gathered about to listen. It was plain that they understood that this was a white man's war; their great, grave, watching faces showed it. Young squaws, half-hooded in their shawls, looked on with bright eyes;

a boy who had been sitting out on the steps
playing a pipe, stopped his music, and came
in; the aged Pounded Meat, wrapped in scarlet and shrunk with years to the appearance
of a dried apple, watched with eyes that still
had in them the primal fire of life; tall in a
corner stood the silver-haired High Bear,
watching, too. Did they understand the white
man's war lying behind the complacent smile
of Horacles and the dangerous smile of the
lounging Scipio? The red man is grave when
war is in question; all the Indians were perfectly still.

"Wish you boys could be there to give me
a good send-off," continued Horacles.

The pipe-playing Indian boy must have
caught some flash of something beneath
Scipio's smile, for his eyes went to Scipio's
pistol—but it returned to Scipio's face.

Horacles spoke on. "Fine line of fresh
Eastern goods, dry goods, candies, and—hee-
hee!—free lunch. Mr. Le Moyne, I want to
thank you publicly for that idea."

"Y'u're welcome to it. Guess I'll hardly be
over to-morrow, though. With such a compet-
itor as you, I expect I'll have to stay with my
job and hustle."

"Ah, well," simpered Horacles, "I couldn't

have done it by myself. My uncle—say, boys!'' (Horacles in the elation of victory now melted to pure good-will) ''do come see me to-morrow. It's all business, this, you know. There's no hard feelings?''

The pipe boy couldn't help looking at the pistol again.

''Not a feeling!'' cried Scipio. And he clapped Horacles between his little round shoulders. With head on one side, he looked down along his lengthy, jocular nose at Horacles for a moment. Then his eye shone upon the company like the edge of a knife—and they laughed at him because he was laughing so contagiously at them; a soft laugh, like the fall of moccasins. Often the Indian will join, like a child in mirth which he does not comprehend. High Bear's smile shone from his corner at young Scipio, whom he fancied so much that he had offered him his fourteenth daughter to wed as soon as his leg should be well. But Scipio had sorrowfully explained to the father that he was already married— which was true, but which I fear would in former days have proved no impediment to him.

''Hey!'' said High Bear now, to Scipio. ''New store. Pretty good. Heap cheap.''

"Yes, High Bear. Heap cheap. You savvy why?"

With a long arm and an outstretched finger, Scipio suddenly pointed to Horacles. At this the Virginian's hitherto unchanging face wakened to curiosity and attention. Scipio was now impressively and mysteriously nodding at the silver-haired chief in his bright, green blanket, and his long, fringed, yellow, soft buckskins.

"No savvy," said High Bear, after a pause, with a tinge of caution. He had followed Scipio's pointing finger to where Horacles was happily practising a trick with a glass and a silver dollar behind the counter.

"Heap cheap," repeated Scipio, "because" (here he leaned close to High Bear and whispered) "because his uncle medicine-man. He big medicine-man, too."

High Bear's eyes rested for a moment on Horacles. Then he shook his head. "Ah, nah," he grunted. "He not medicine-man. He fall off horse. He no catch horse. My little girl catch him. Ah, nah!" High Bear laughed profusely at "Sippo's" joke. "Sippo" was the Indian's English name for their vivacious friend. In their own language they called him something complimentary in several syllables,

but it was altogether too intimate and too
plain-spoken for me to repeat aloud. Into his
whisper Scipio now put more electricity.
"He's big medicine-man," he hissed again,
and he drilled his bleached blue eye into the
brown one of the savage. "See him now!" He
stretched out a vibrating finger.

It was a pack of cards that Horacles was
lightly manipulating. He fluttered it open in
the air and fluttered it shut again, drawing it
out like a concertina and pushing it flat like
an opera hat—nor did a card fall to the
ground.

High Bear watched it hard; but soon High
Bear laughed. "He pretty good," he declared.
"All same tin-horn monte-man. I see one
Miles City."

"Maybe monte-man medicine-man, too,"
suggested Scipio.

"Ah, nah!" said High Bear. Yet nevertheless Scipio saw him shoot one or two more
doubtful glances at Horacles as that happy
clerk continued his activities.

Horacles had an audience (which he liked),
and he held his audience—and who could help
liking that? The bucks and squaws watched
him, sometimes nudging one another, and they
smiled and grunted their satisfaction at his

news. Cheaper prices was something which
their primitive minds could take in as well as
any of us.

"Why you not sell cheap like him?" they
asked their friend "Sippo." "We stay then.
Not go his store." This was the burden of
their chorus, soft, laughing, a little mocking,
floating among them like a breeze, voice after
voice:—

"We like buy everything you, we like buy
everything cheap."

"You make cheap, we buy heap shirts."

"Buy heap tobacco."

"Heap cartridge."

"You not sell cheap, we go."

"Ah!"

The chorus laughed like pleased children.

Scipio looked at them solemnly. He explained how much he would like to sell cheap,
if only he were a medicine-man like Horacles.

"You medicine-man?" they asked the assistant clerk.

"Yes," said Horacles, pleased. "I big medicine-man."

"Ah, nah!" The soft, mocking words ran
among them like the flight of a moth.

Soon with their hoods over their heads they
began to go home on their ponies, blanketed,

feathered, many-colored, moving and dispersing wide across the sage-brush of their far-scattered tepees.

High Bear lingered last. For a long while he had been standing silent and motionless. When the chorus spoke he had not; when the chorus laughed he had not. Now his head moved; he looked about him and saw that for a moment he was alone in a way. He saw the Virginian reading a newspaper, and his friend "Sippo" bending down and attending to his leg. Horacles had gone into an inner room. Left on the counter lay the pack of cards. High Bear went quickly to the cards, touched them, lifted them, set them down, and looked about him again. But the Virginian was reading still, and Scipio was still bent down, having some trouble with his boot. High Bear looked at the cards, shook his head sceptically, laughed a little, grunted once, and went out where his pony was tied. As he was throwing his soft buckskin leg over the saddle, there was Scipio's head thrust out of the door and nodding strangely at him.

"Good night, High Bear. He big medicine-man."

High Bear gave a quick slash to his pony, and galloped away into the dusk.

Then Scipio limped back into the store, sank into the first chair he came to, and doubled over. The Virginian looked up from his paper at this mirth, scowled, and turned back to his reading. If he was to be "left out" of the joke, he would make it plain that he was not in the least interested in it.

Scipio now sat up straight, bursting to share what was in his mind; but he instantly perceived how it was with the Virginian. At this he redoubled his silent symptoms of delight. In a moment Horacles had come back from the inner room with his hair wet with ornamental brushing.

"Well, Horacles," began Scipio in the voice of a purring cat, "I expect y'u have me beat."

The flattered clerk could only nod and show his bright, false teeth.

"Y'u have me beat," repeated Scipio. "Y'u have for a fact."

"Not you, Mr. Le Moyne. It's not you I'm making war on. I do hope there's no hard feelings—"

"Not a feelin', Horacles! How can y'u entertain such an idea?" Scipio shook him by the hand and smiled like an angel at him—a fallen angel. "What's the use of me keepin' this store open to-morrow? Nobody'll be here to spend a cent. Guess I'll shut up, Horacles, and come watch the Injuns all shoppin' like Christmas over to your place.''

The Virginian sustained his indifference, and added to Scipio's pleasure. But during breakfast the Virginian broke down.

"Reckon you're ready to start to-day?" he said.

"Start? Where for?"

"Sunk Creek, y'u fool! Where else?"

"I'm beyond y'u! I'm sure beyond y'u for once!" screeched Scipio, beating his crutch on the floor.

"Oh, eat your grub, y'u fool."

"I'd have told y'u last night," said Scipio, remorselessly, "only y'u were so awful anxious not to *be* told."

As the Virginian drove him across the sage-brush, not to Sunk Creek, but to the new store, the suspense was once more too much for the Southerner's curiosity. He pulled up the horses as the inspiration struck him.

"You're going to tell the Indians you'll under-sell him!" he declared, over-hastily.

"Oh, drive on, y'u fool," said Scipio.

The baffled Virginian grinned. "I'll throw you out," he said, "and break all your laigs and bones and things fresh."

"I wish Uncle was going to be there," said
Scipio.

Nearly everybody else was there: the
Agent, bearing his ill fortune like a philoso-
pher; some officers from the Post, and the
doctor; some enlisted men, blue-legged with
yellow stripes; civilians male and female,
honorable and shady; and then the Indians.
Wagons were drawn up, ponies stood about,
the littered plain was populous. Horacles
moved behind the counter, busy and happy;
his little mustache was combed, his ornamental hair was damp. He smiled and talked, and
handled and displayed his abundance: the
bright calicoes, the shining knives, the clean
six-shooters and rifles, the bridles, the fishing-
tackle, the gum-drops and chocolates—all his
plenty and its cheapness.

Squaws and bucks young and old thronged
his establishment, their soft footfalls and
voices made a gentle continuous sound, while
their green and yellow blankets bent and
stood straight as they inspected and pur-
chased. High Bear held an earthen crock with
a luxury in it—a dozen of fresh eggs. "Hey!"
he said when he saw his friend "Sippo" enter. "Heap cheap." And he showed the eggs
to Scipio. He cherished the crock with one

hand and arm while with the other hand he
helped himself to the free lunch.

To Scipio Horacles ''extended'' a special
welcome; he made it ostentatious in order
that all the world might know how perfectly
absent ''hard feelings'' were. And Scipio on
his side wore openly the radiance of brother-
hood and well-wishing. He went about admiring everything, exclaiming now and then over
the excellence of the goods, or the cheapness
of their price. His presence was soon no
longer a cause of curiosity, and they forgot
to watch him—all of them except the Virginian. The hours passed on, the little fires,
where various noon meals were cooked, burnt
out, satisfied individuals began to depart
after an entertaining day, the Agent himself
was sauntering toward his horse.

''What's your hurry?'' said Scipio.

''Well, the show is over,'' said the Agent.

''Oh, no, it ain't. Horacles is goin' to entertain us a whole lot.''

''Better stay,'' said the Virginian.

The Agent looked from one to the other.
Then he spoke anxiously. ''I don't want anything done to Horacles.''

''Nothing will be done,'' stated Scipio.

Very curious and but half re-assured, the
Agent stayed. The magnetic current of ex-

pectancy passed, none could say how, through
the assembled people. No one departed after
this, and the mere loitering of spectators
turned to waiting. Particularly expectant was
the Virginian, and this he betrayed by me-
chanically droning in his strongest accent a
little song that bore no reference to the present occasion:—

> "Of all my fatheh's familee
> I love myself the baist,
> And if Gawd will just look afteh me
> The devil may take the raist."

The sun grew lower. The world outside was
still full of light, but dimness had begun its
subtle pervasion of the store. Horacles
thanked the Indians and every one for their
generous patronage on this his opening day,
and intimated that it was time to close. Scipio
rushed up and whispered to him:—

"My goodness, Horacles! You ain't going
to send your friends home like that?"

Horacles was taken aback. "Why," he
stammered, "what's wrong?"

"Where's your vanishing handkerchief,
Horacles? Get it out and entertain 'em some.
Show you're grateful. Where's that trick dol-
lar? Get 'em quick.—I tell you," he declaimed
aloud to the Indians, "he big medicine-man.
Make come. Make go. You no see. Nobody

see. Nobody see. Make jack-rabbit in hat—''

"I couldn't to-night," simpered Horacles. "Needs preparation, you know." And he winked at Scipio.

Scipio struggled upon the counter, and stood up above their heads to finish his speech. "No jack-rabbit this time," he said.

"Ah, nah!" laughed the Indians. "No catch um."

"Yes, catch um any time. Catch anything. Make anything. Make all this store"—Scipio moved his arms about—"that's how make heap cheap. See that!" He stopped dramatically and clasped his hands together. Horacles tossed a handkerchief in the air, caught it, shut his hand upon it with a kneading motion, and opened the hand empty. "His fingers swallow it, all same mouth!" shouted Scipio. "He big medicine-man. You see. Now other hand spit out." But Horacles varied the trick. Success and the staring crowd elated him; he was going to do his best. He opened both hands empty, felt about him in the air, clutched space suddenly, and drew two silver dollars from it. Then he threw them back into space, again felt about for them in the air, made a dive at High Bear's eggs, and brought handkerchief and dollars out of them.

"Ho!" went High Bear, catching his breath. He backed away from the reach of Horacles. He peered down into the crock among his eggs. Horacles whispered to Scipio:—

"Keep talking till I'm ready."

"Oh, I'll talk. Go get ready quick,—High Bear, what I tell you?" But High Bear's eye was now fixedly watching the door through which Horacles had withdrawn; he did not listen as Scipio proceeded. "What I tell everybody? He do handkerchief. He do dollar. He do heap more. See me. I no can do like him. I not medicine-man. I throw handkerchief and dollar in the air, look! See! they tumble on floor no good,—thank you, my kind noble friend from Virginia, you pick my fool dollar and my fool handkerchief up for me, *muy pronto*. Oh, thank you, black-haired, green-eyed son of Dixie, you have the manners of a queen, but I no medicine-man, I shall never turn a skunk into a watermelon, I innocent, I young, I helpless babe, I suck bottle when I can get it. Fire and water will not obey me. Old man Makes-the-Thunder does not know my name and address. He spit on me Wednesday night last, and there are no dollars in this man's hair." (The Virginian winced beneath Scipio's vicious snatch at his scalp, and the Agent and the doctor retired to a dark corner and laid their heads in each other's waistcoats.) "Ha! he comes! Big medicine-man comes. See him, High Bear! His father, his mother, his aunts all twins, he ninth dog-pup in three sets of triplets, and the great white Ram-of-the-Mountains fed him on punkin-seed.—Sick 'em, Horacles.''

The burning eye of High Bear now blazed with distended fascination, riveted upon Horacles, whom it never left. Darkness was gathering in the store.

"Hand all same foot," shouted Scipio, with gestures, "mouth all same hand. Can eat fire. Can throw ear mile off and listen you talk." Here Horacles removed a dollar from the hair of High Bear's fourteenth daughter, threw it into one boot, and brought it out of the other. The daughter screamed and burrowed behind her sire. All the Indians had drawn close together, away from the counter, while Scipio on top of the counter talked high and low, and made gestures without ceasing. "Hand all same mouth. Foot all same head. Take off head, throw it out window, it jump in door. See him, see big medicine-man!" And Scipio gave a great shriek.

A gasp went among the Indians; red fire was blowing from the jaws of Horacles. It

ceased, and after it came slowly, horribly, a
long red tongue, and riding on the tongue's
end glittered a row of teeth. There was a
crash upon the floor. It was High Bear's
crock. The old chief was gone. Out of the
door he flew, his blanket over his face, and up
on his horse he sprang, wildly beating the animal. Squaws and bucks flapped after him like
poultry, rushing over the ground, leaping on
their ponies, melting away into the dusk. In a
moment no sign of them was left but the broken eggs, oozing about on the deserted floor.

The white men there stood tearful, dazed,
and weak with laughter.

" 'Happy Teeth' should be his name,'' said
the Virginian. "It sounds Injun.'' And
Happy Teeth it was.

But Horacles did not remain long in the
neighborhood after he realized what he had
done; for never again did an Indian enter, or
even come near, that den of flames and magic.
They would not even ride past it; they circled
it widely. The idle merchandise that filled it
was at last bought by the Agent at a reduction.

"Well," said Scipio bashfully to the Agent,
"I'd have sure hated to hand y'u back a
ruined business. But he'll never understand
Injuns.''

II

THE cabin on Spit-Cat Creek lies lonely among the high pastures, and looks down to further loneliness across many slanting levels of pine-tops. These descend successively in smooth, odorous, evergreen miles until they reach the open valley. Here runs the stage road, if you can discern it, from the railway to the continuously jubilant cow-town of Likely, Wyoming; and here, when viewed from the cabin through a field-glass you can readily distinguish an antelope from a stone in the clear atmosphere which commonly prevails. The windows of the cabin are three, and looking in through any of them you can see the stove, the table, and the ingenuous structure which does duty as a bed. During the season of snow, from November until May, the cabin, in the days of which I speak, was dwelt in by no one; while through the open weather some person of honesty and resource would be sent thither from the headquarters ranch on Sunk Creek two or three

times, to stay no longer than his duties re-
quired, and to come back with his report as
soon as they should be performed. Such a
man would live here with canned food and the
small stove, seldom having other company
than his own, and, if he had ears for the
music of nature, the singing pines would often
companion him, he could hear now and again
some unseen bird crying as it passed among
them, and always the voice of Spit-Cat. This
stream foamed by the cabin to fall and wander deviously away into the great, distant
silence of the mountains. Likely was eighteen
miles distant, and to this place the man could
ride in four hours by a recently discovered
trail, which was the shorter one, and followed
the smaller tributary stream of Spit-Kitten;
and sometimes the man did so ride for his
mail, or for more canned food, or for a game
of chance and female company, in the continuously jubilant cow-town of Likely, Wyoming.

Upon a midday in June, had you secretly
peered through any of the windows in the
cabin, you could have seen a seated man,
tightly curved over the table and apparently
dying in convulsions brought on by poison;
for the signs of a newly finished meal were
near him. There was a coffee-pot, and a dish

of bacon, and three quarters of a pie. But it was merely Scipio Le Moyne endeavoring to write a letter; and no task more excruciating was known to this young man.

"Dear friend," he had begun, "i got no dictionery, but—"

At this point a heavy blot had intervened as he was changing the personal pronoun into a capital I.

"Oh, gosh!" he sighed, and for a while could spell no more. He sat back, staring at the paper. "It's not to a girl," he presently muttered. "I guess I'll not start a fresh sheet." And while the perspiring Scipio laid his nose to his pen and dragged himself onward from word to word, a bad old gentleman with a black coat and a white beard was coming stealthily up from the valley through the thick pines. He was still some miles away, and he meant to look in at one of the windows, and regulate his conduct according to what he should then see. He was by no means sure that Scipio had what he wanted, which was as much money as he could get, or any fraction thereof; but he had a shrewd suspicion that he could ascertain this without any extreme use of deadly weapons.

Scipio Le Moyne was making his first stay

in the Spit-Cat cabin, and in his mind there welled a complacency not to be justified; for when a thick roll of money is in a man's trousers, and the man's trousers are upon the man, and the man is writing a letter at a table, you see at once how unsafe the money is if the man's six-shooter is lying out of reach on the bed behind him. It should be hanging at his hip, or in the armhole of his waistcoat, or stuck elsewhere handily about his immediate person. And so it would have been on any ordinary day of Scipio's life; but alas! on this day he was writing a letter, and was therefore not quite accountable. There were many things that he did not enjoy—cooking for example, or a bucking pony, or gun trouble in a saloon; but these worries he could usually meet. The only crisis which invariably disturbed him—except, of course, having to talk to Eastern ladies when they visited the Judge's ranch—was to be face to face with ink and a pen. After his midday meal this noon he had reclined upon his bed, putting off the hateful moment. Thus recumbent he had unbuckled his belt for comfort and got none, for the letter made him restless. At length, with a mind absent from everything save the coming ink and pen, he had gone to them, forgetting his revolver among the rumpled blankets.

Complacency welled in his mind because of errands accomplished. He had been trusted, and he had a pride in it deeper than any words he was willing to utter, and a gratitude which he would express by inference alone. He would do everything that they had given him to do so well that it could not be done better; that is how he would thank his friend, the Sunk Creek foreman, for giving him his chance to show his abilities—and his radical honesty. (Scipio was not in the least honest on the surface.) He would take no man's word for an inch of the work that he had been sent to oversee on both sides of the mountain; he would visit the various camps when he was not expected; every cow to be bought should be bought on his own inspection and not on the seller's assurances. But these trusts were little compared with the heavy wages that he was carrying to pay off certain men when certain work should be finished. He had hoped to be rid of this at once, but late snows and high water had delayed the work.

Scipio Le Moyne was among the newcomers at the headquarters ranch on Sunk Creek. His character had not yet been tested by a year's

scrutiny. He was known to ride and rope well,
and to cook indifferently, and to return from
town having behaved himself less ill than the
worst; but Judge Henry had drawn back from
putting in his hands a temptation so potent as
the wages. Much ready money is a burning
argument for a disappearance. To these cautious sentiments of the Judge his foreman had
replied scarcely more than "I have studied
Scipio mighty thorough." To Scipio himself,
the friend for whose character he was thus
pledging his good judgment, he merely remarked, "Stay with the money."

"Stay with it!" exclaimed Scipio, nearly
overcome by his feelings. He wanted to hug
the foreman; and lest his eyes should betray
something, he narrowed them to a wicked slit,
and put on the disguise of jocularity. "If y'u
say so, I'll stay with it till I come home with
it."

The usually sharp-witted foreman was at
a loss.

"Sure!" Scipio explained. "I'll pay the
boys what they're owed, and take 'em into
Likely and win it back off 'em. Why, it's the
kind of plan y'u might think of yourself."

"You're cert'nly shameless," murmured
the foreman.

"So my enemies all say," retorted Scipio. And he departed to Spit-Cat Creek.

And now, having done well most things he was sent to do, his heart was so grateful to his friend that he would conquer his distaste for the pen, and write a long letter without a single word of thanks in it—the thanks would merely be between every line. The truly heavy load of responsibility was still with him, but safe with him; that money would go into the hands of the men at the Flat Iron outfit to-morrow, and surprise them. Had he not been adroit? No one suspected he was the paymaster. Visiting Likely once for his mail and some supplies, he had been obliged to spend the night there. His prudence as to whisky and general abstemiousness of conduct that night might point, he feared, to the fact that he carried money he was "staying with." He even felt a certain observation to attend his movements. He therefore began to speak deceitfully to the company he sat among. Had anybody else, he inquired, been through here from Sunk Creek? Nobody else had, it appeared; and Scipio smoked for a while.

"Well," he remarked at length, with a certain gloom, like one who speaks from an offended heart, "a man don't enjoy bein' mistrusted. Not if there's never been nothing to justify it." He said no more, waiting for some one to draw the desired inference from this utterance.

After a matter of some five minutes the inference was appreciated, and he received a counter-offer, so to speak, a trifle too obviously aimed. "Them hands at the Flat Iron," said the offerer, "has most finished their job, ain't they?"

"I don't know about them," said Scipio, keeping in the land of inference. "I've finished mine, I know." Then, after a proper pause and with proper bitterness, he finished: "If folks can't trust me they can't hire me."

It was lightly handled, and it did its work in Likely. All Likely gossiped next day about how Judge Henry would not let Scipio handle the Flat Iron money, and how Scipio let his feelings be shown too plain for self-respect— all Likely, save one close observer. The old gentleman with the black coat and the white beard thought that it was odd in Scipio to behave so carefully during his night in town, odd and interesting to drink nothing and go to bed early in the hotel. "That kind don't," he said to himself; "not usually when they're mad at their employer and goin' to quit their job.'' The old gentleman did not gossip, but grew thoughtful. One morning he got on his old pink mare, and took a quiet trail for Spit-Cat. He thought he knew the way, but lost himself, and luckily met a man on the stage road who directed him up the old, established trail. Or rather, it was lucky that he lost himself, else he would have arrived before Scipio had unbuckled his pistol and forgotten everything in the world but this letter he was knee-deep in.

"*Dear friend* I got no dictionery but if any of my spelling raises your suspicions you can borrow a dictionery at your end and theirby correct my statements which are otherwise garranteed to be strictly accurite. Hope you are well I am same. Have a good notion not to sine this for you will know my tracks without more information. Well buisniss first and I will try run in a little pleasure for you if my nerve holds out but that blot will tell you I am not myself just now. You said I was shameless but you are dead wrong about me. To think of the way you lied to those poor boys about the frogs has made me blush in bed after many a day when my own concience was at piece. I have looked after the new ditches I had to attend to them a whole lot they are all

right now but they were not the young yellow-
leg who calls himself a civil engineer I guess
becaus he looks at a grade through a machine
on three sticks instead of with his naked eye
was making trouble. He was arranging for
the water from Crow Canyon to run up hill.
We got it started the right way yesterday but
that civil engineer does too much fingering
with his pencil to suit me he has a whole box
full of sums in arrithmetic. The fences are
satisfactory. I was obliged to turn half the
cattle back the man thought I was one of those
who do not know a cow when they see one but
he has gone home realizing his poor judgment.
And now that is all except I am paying off
the extra hands at the Flat Iron outfit to-morrow or next day sure and now for pleasure as
my hand has got limbered up wonderful and
no longer obliged to blast out every word
with giant powder like I had to all around the
start where you see those blots. I guess the
words are going to get to chasing each other
off this pen before I am through telling you
something.

"I have noticed a thing. Be the first to tell
a joke on yourself it deadens the blow. Well
Honey Wiggin has found out about this so I
am going to hurry up and get ahead of his

news. Likely is the town here as you know and
twenty hours is still the record for driving to
it from the railroad but there is a new trail
from here to Likely by Spit-Kitten it saves an
hour so I am living an hour nearer the fashion
than you told me I would be when you gave
me this job. But it was by no means to be
fashionable that I had to go over to Likely
though it is a good place for a man who wants
to and this cabin is not fashionable a little bit
but my flour gave out. The last of it was eat
up by Honey Wiggin who stopped here one
night and told me about the trail by Spit-Kitten witch he claimed was easy except in one
place by what they call the Little Pasture.
You come on the fence on the side hill up
among the trees where they have been cut
down some and Honey said follow the fence a
good ways maybe three miles he thought but
not more and you would see the place where
the trail took off down the hill through the
same kind of trees pretty thin growing and
pines mostly till you would come to the edge
and see the town down below about half an
hour more riding. Honey went over the
mountain to Flat Iron and I caught up my
horse and started for Likely. The trail was
all right unless for a horse packed heavy and

I did not hurry any for I knew I had the night
to put in in town and I was in no haste to get
there because I could have no enjoyment when
I did on account of the money. I was invited
a lot when I got there but though I have been
going to bed the same day I got up for many
weeks I was taking no risk. But that is not my
point it is the Little Pasture I want to speak
of. It got shady while I was following the
fence which I struck all right but I did not
mind and I was studying up something to tell
any folks that might inquire about the money
for Flat Iron for I have to practiss lying I am
not quick at it like you. Well sir I went along
getting up some remarks and then picking out
them I considered to be the most promissing
but after a while I says to myself it must be
most three miles I have come along this fence.
But Honey Wiggin is not special close about
distances, and so I went along rejecting some
of the remarks I had picked out and putting
stronger ones in their place and pretty soon I
knew I must have come five miles anyway for
Japan can walk three miles an hour and I had
looked at my watch. I made Japan lope and
then I made him gallup and then something
struck me like a flash and I got off him and
tied my hankerchef to the fence and me and

Japan gallupped like we was both crazy and it was not twenty minnits till we came round to my hankerchef again. I expect the pasture is three miles round but cannot say how many times I circled her. I struck out for myself then and come to another fence and that was the one Honey meant, only he says now he told me to look out and not take the first fence.

"In Likely I went to bed the same day I got up and I slept in my pants with the money and can say I will be glad when—"

Here Scipio Le Moyne looked up from his letter, for the old gentleman stood in the door and wished him good morning. It was not morning, but let that go. The old gentleman had taken his observations through the window behind Scipio and had been much pleased to notice the six-shooter among the blankets. He had observed everything: the pie, the letter, all things inside the cabin, and also that outside the cabin Scipio's horse was grazing in the little field, and therefore not instantly serviceable. His own animal he had tied to a tree a little distance within the timber.

"Good morning," he said.

Scipio's entire inward arrangements gave a monstrous leap, but his outward start was very slight. "Hello, Uncle Pasco!" said he cheerfully. "Are y'u lost?" And he sat in his chair quite still.

Uncle Pasco stood blinking in his usual way. "No," he returned. "Not lost. Just off trappin'. That's what." His voice was an old man's, dry and chirping, and his sentences proceeded in short hops. He had seen Scipio's one-quarter inch of movement, and he read that movement with admirable insight: it had been a quickly arrested and choked impulse to get to those blankets. And Scipio had done some reading, too. He saw Uncle Pasco's eye measuring distances, and he could discern no sign whatever of pistol upon the old gentleman. This rendered him extremely cautious, and his thoughts worked at a remarkable speed. Uncle Pasco did not have to think so quickly, for he had begun his meditations in Likely several days ago, and they were all finished as far as they could be up to the present juncture. Even the most ripened strategist must leave some moves to be determined by the fluctuations of the battle.

"Been off trappin'," repeated Uncle Pasco.

"What luck?" Scipio inquired.

"Poor. Poor. Beaver gettin' cleaned out of this country. That's what."

"Better sit down and eat," said Scipio. "Take your coat off and stay awhile."

Uncle Pasco's glance rested on the pie a moment, and then upon Scipio's ink-covered sheets. "M—well," he said doubtfully, for Scipio's ease had now put him in doubt, "I got to get back to Likely. Pie looks good. Pie like mother made. That's what. M—well, you're busy. Guess you want to write your letter."

Scipio now looked at his letter, and drew inspiration from it, a forlorn hope of inspiration. "Why, you don't need to start for Likely so soon," he remarked with a persuasive whine. "What was the use in stoppin' at all? Eat the balance of the pie and take the new trail—if your packs are not loaded heavy."

"Spit-Kitten?" said Uncle Pasco.

"Yep," said Scipio. "Saves an hour."

"Ain't been over it," said Uncle Pasco.

"Can't miss it," said Scipio. "Your pack's light?"

"M—well," answered Uncle Pasco, doubtfully, "fairly light."

"Sit down," said Scipio. "I'll tell y'u about the trail while you're eatin' the pie." He made as if to rise and offer the only chair in the room to Uncle Pasco. This brought Uncle Pasco immediately to his side.

"Keep a-sittin'," the old gentleman urged. "Keep a-sittin', and draw me a map. That's what. Map of Spit-Kitten."

"Here," began Scipio, wriggling his pen across a blank sheet, "runs Spit-Cat. This here cross is this cabin. Stream's runnin' this way. Understand?"

"That's plain," said Uncle Pasco.

"Here," and Scipio wriggled his pen at right angles to the first wriggle, "comes Spit-Kitten into the main creek—right above this cabin. See? Well. Now." Scipio began dotting lines. "You follow the little creek up, so. Then you cross over to the left bank, so. And you go right up out of a little cañon (you can't if your packs is heavy loaded, for it's awful steep and slippery for pretty near a hundred yards) and you come out on top clear going—gosh! I've got to take another sheet of paper—well, now y'u go down easy a mile or two and keep swinging to your right, and about here"—Scipio now sprinkled some points on the paper—"the trees begin gettin' scattery and you look out for a fence on your left. You follow that fence for—well, I'd not say whether it's three miles or four—it's that noo pasture the Seventy-six outfit calls their Little Pasture, and before y'u come to the corner where there's a gate by a gushin' creek

I don't know the name of, you'll notice the hill goin' down to your right all over good grass and mighty few trees, and if it's dark you'll see the lights of the town below and the trail takes off right about where you'll be standing this way'' (Scipio scratched an arrow), ''and don't y'u mind if it looks like a little-worn trail, for that's the way it is, and y'u can't miss it on that hillside. See?''

''That's plain as day,'' said Uncle Pasco, accepting the two sheets of the map and sliding them into his own pocket. He still stood beside Scipio, irresolutely, considering the lumpy appearance of Scipio's pocket. A handkerchief with a bag of tobacco might produce such a bulge.

''Fine day,'' said Scipio. ''Better stay a while.''

''Good weather right along now,'' said Uncle Pasco.

''Time it was,'' said Scipio, ''after the wettin' the month of May gave us. Boys doin' anything in town lately?''

''Oh, gay, gay,'' returned Uncle Pasco. And he ran a pistol against Scipio's head. ''Out with it,'' he commanded. ''Cough up.''

It is possible, in these circumstances, to refuse to cough, and to perform instead some rapid athletics which result in a bullet-hole in the wall or ceiling, to be forever after pointed to. But the odds are so heavy that the hole will be in neither the wall nor the ceiling that many people of undoubted valor have found coughing more discreet. Scipio coughed.

"Uncle Pasco," said he gracefully, "I didn't know you were that artistic."

Uncle Pasco now marched to the bed, and appropriated Scipio's pistol. "Just for the present," he explained.

"Uncle Pasco," resumed Scipio, mild as a dove, and never stirring from his chair, "you have learned me something to-day. It's expensive education. I'll not say it ain't. But I'm goin' to tell y'u where I went wrong. I'd ought to have acted more careless in Likely that night. I'd ought to have taken a whirl somewheres. Bein' so quiet exposed my hand to y'u. But, see here, I had everybody fooled but you."

"You're a kid," responded Uncle Pasco, but with indulgence. "You be good. Keep a-sittin' right there. Pie like mother made." And with the pie in one hand and his pistol in the other he made a comfortable lunch.

"It *was* my over-carefulness, warn't it?"

persisted Scipio. "I have sure paid y'u good to know!"

"You're a kid," Uncle Pasco, with unchanged indulgence, repeated. "You'll do in time. Keep studying seasoned men. That's what." And he finished his meal. "You'll find your six-shooter in the place where I'll put it."

The old gentleman opened the door, and, leaving Scipio in the chair, walked briskly by the corral into the trees and mounted his old pink mare. From the door of the cabin Scipio watched him amble away along the banks of Spit-Cat.

"Pie like mother made!" he muttered. "You patch-sewed bread-basket! Why, you fringy-panted walking delegate, I'll agitate your system till your back teeth are chewin' your own sweetbreads!" He seized up a rope and began walking to where his horse was pasturing. "I could forgive him takin' the money," he continued. "He outplayed me. But—" Scipio was silent for a few yards, and then, "Pie like mother made!" he burst out again.

The afternoon was growing late and shadow was ascending among the thin pines by the Little Pasture. Uncle Pasco, ambling easily

along, counted his money, and slapped his bad
old leg with joy. With all those dollars he
could render the next several months more
than comfortable. He consulted Scipio's map,
and here, sure enough, he came to the fence
just as Scipio said he would; that fence he was
to follow for three miles, perhaps, or four.
Uncle Pasco slapped his leg again, and gave
a horrid, unconscientious cackle. He hung
Scipio's pistol on a post of the fence and rode
on, while pleasing thoughts of San Francisco
and champagne filled his mind. After him at a
nicely set interval, came Scipio along the trail.
All worked with the agreeable precision of a
clock. Scipio recovered his pistol, and after
tying his horse out of sight a little way down
the hill, he ran back and sat snug behind a
tree close to the fence, waiting. He looked at
his watch. "It took Japan and me twenty
minutes to go around at a gallop," he observed. "Uncle Pasco ain't goin' half that
fast." Scipio continued to wait with his six-
shooter ready. In due time he pricked up his
ears and rose upon his feet behind the tree.
Next, he stepped forth with his smile of an
angel—but a fallen angel.

"Pie like mother made," he remarked mu-
sically.   .   .   .

Why tell of Uncle Pasco's cruel surprise? It is not known if he had gone round the fence more than once; but the town of Likely saw the dreadful condition of his clothes as he rode in that night. It was almost no clothes.

At that hour Scipio was finishing his letter to the foreman:—

"—this risponsibillity is shed," had been the unwritten fragment of his sentence when it was cut short, and he now completed it, and went on:—

"Quite a little thing has took place just now about that money. Don't jump for I am staying with it as you said to and I am liable to be staying with it as long as necessary but an old hobo held me up and got it off me and kept it for most three hours when I got it back off the old fool. I would not have throwed him around like I did if he had been content to lift the cash but he had to insult me too said I was pie and next time he'll know a man should be civil no matter what his employment is.

"I have noticed another thing. To shoot strait always go to bed the same day you get up and to think strait use same pollicy.

"Your friend,
"SCIPIO LE MOYNE.
"P.S.   I am awful oblidged to you."

III

FORCE, as you may know, is like the King, and never dies. It endlessly transmits itself through the same or some other shape. Drop a stone in a pond, and the wave-rings may seem to expire as they widen, but they do not; through friction or impact or something, they merely become invisible. You can stop a cannon-ball, but you cannot kill its speed; its speed is immortal and undergoes instant resurrection, taking the new shape of heat. The cannon-ball becomes red hot and sends heat waves off into infinity. Scientific men have told you all this as they have told me and I should not wonder if the scientific men were right.

I. The Storing of the Energy

ONCE upon a time the army had a wet-nurse instead of a secretary of war. The nurse fed our soldiers upon speeches, milk-and-sugar speeches, all over the country. He told them he was going to right their wrongs. Now, as they didn't know that they had any wrongs,

61

this both surprised and pleased them. They
liked to hear him inform them that it was they
who from the first had won our battles upon
land and sea. "Who" (he would ask rhetor-
ically), "who endured the bitter cold, the
frozen snow, at Valley Forge?" And as they
hadn't the slightest idea, what more agreeable
than to learn it was themselves? "Let us
honor George Washington" (he would ex-
claim), "let us not forget that great and good
man! but let us remember also the honest
soldier without whose aid George Washington
could never have durriven the Burritish ty-
rant from our beloved shores of furreedom!"

He always spoke of the "honest" soldier,
and therefore the average enlisted man very
naturally felt that somehow George Washington, Andrew Jackson and Ulysses Grant were
all well enough in their way, but that you
must keep your eye on them, and that the
Secretary was the man to put them in their
proper place. The Secretary quite rightly
omitted to state that generals are apt to carry
a responsibility which would iron the average
enlisted man flatter than a pair of pressed
trousers; he omitted this statement because it
would have been the whole truth, and the
whole truth is often very tiresome, particu-

larly for a politician. Do not, as you read this, think evil of the Secretary; he had a large family of daughters and sons with whom he was frequently photographed, seated on the vine-clad porch of the old white homestead, and these photographs were at once widely given to the public press. Moreover, his private life was known to be chaste by every lady in the land, though how they ascertained this I am at a loss to explain. He was also a highly gifted man; gifted with the voice that matches a political frock-coat. At will he could make this so impressive, that if he remarked it was a fine day, for the time of year, it convinced the audience that something of the utmost importance had been announced. He was gifted, too, with a face impervious to vulgar scrutiny, and he had the most deeply religious chinbeard in Apple-Jack county. I have already mentioned that he possessed the gift of tears, when such phenomenon was timely, and besides all these things, he owned some extensive salt-marshes on a bay. These were too wet for private persons to buy, but he was going to be happy to sell them to the government for a naval station when he should be Senator, after his present office had expired. Meanwhile he went about busily with his basket, collecting popularity from the humblest dumping lot.

If there was one kind of audience that the Secretary liked above all others, it was an audience of fresh, bright, brave, young recruits. He missed no chance to tell them so. Their earnest faces, he was apt to say if there was a flag anywhere in sight, stirred his heart more, much more than the stars upon Old Glory waving yonder. Then he would point to Old Glory, and get results from the gallery as satisfactory as any actor could wish. Indeed, the Secretary could have made the drama as lucrative as he made politics. He could tell a story and make you laugh, tell another and make you cry, and a really excellent second-rate actor was lost in him.

Recruits after his own heart sat close before him one afternoon at McPherson gathered from various Southern States.

"Let those young men come up front!" he had commanded from the platform in his deepest frock-coat basso. "Let them see me and let me see them. We understand each other, for we are comrades."

Accordingly, the recruits occupied the front benches, while the mustache of Captain Stone, who sat in the rear of the hall, began to look

like the back of a dog's neck when the dog is
not pleased. The captain took down one leg
that had been crossed over the other, and began sliding one hand up and down the yellow
stripe of his trousers. To his brother officers
and to his favorite sergeant, Jones, this hand
sliding was another sign, like the singular
behavior of the mustache. Nobody knew
whether it was the hair itself that rose, or
whether he did it with his upper lip; but when
the whole thing stood straight out beyond his
nose, everybody knew at a hundred yards'
range what it meant, no matter how it was
done. It was the hurricane signal and you
steered your course accordingly.

"You never'll get a better captain, Jock,"
Sergeant Jones would often remark to Cor-
poral Cumnor. "But you want to catch his
profile at morning stables. If the muss-tash
is merely standing attention, clear weather's
to be locked for. But if she's deployed in extended order of skirmish-line, don't you go
nowheres without your slicker."

On the present occasion the sergeant was
also in the hall listening to the Secretary. To
him had fallen the responsibility of conducting some of the recruits to Fort Chiricahua
in Arizona, to which post they had been

assigned. Captain Stone was on leave, and had no responsibilities whatever until in a few weeks he should return to that same post after a honeymoon which he and his bride were completing by a visit to the lady's parents. She was a pastor's daughter and played the melodeon.

"We are comrades," repeated the Secretary of War to the recruits, "and that means you and I are going to stand by each other through thick and thin." It sounded so well that the recruits all cheered.

The captain's mustache lifted a couple of hairs more, Sergeant Jones in another part of the hall whispered to himself two words which I cannot repeat, and the Secretary looked about to see if there was a flag anywhere convenient for his popular climax about earnest faces and the stars in Old Glory. But there was no flag, and he therefore selected another of the many strings to his oratorical bow. He gave them his great "What I am for" speech, the speech which had brought the gallery down at Albany on Decoration Day, had caught the crowd at Terre Haute on the Fourth of July, swept Minneapolis on Labor Day and turned Dallas, Texas, hoarse on Washington's Birthday. In

it the Secretary asked "What am I for?" and
then answered the question. He was to watch
over the enlisted man, he was to be his father
and protect him from military tyranny. Superior officers were to cease their despotic
methods. Was this not a republic where one
man was as good as another? The very term
"superior officer" was repugnant to the
American idea, and no offender of any grade
should hide behind it as long as he was Secretary of War. To hear him you would have
supposed that until he stepped into the Cabi-
net the slave under the lash knew a better lot
than the American soldier. To be sure, he did
not always say these remarkable things in the
same way. At Boston, for instance, he would
draw it milder than at Billings, Montana. At
Boston he mentioned other duties of the Secretary of War besides that of tucking the enlisted man in his bed every night; but he
seldom spoke in Boston, because he preferred
a warm, heart-to-heart audience.

He knew at sight that he had one here. His
practised eye ran the recruits over and read
their wholesome vacant up-country faces,
noted their big rosy wrists, appraised their
untrained juicy agricultural shapelessness as
they sat beneath him like rows of cantaloupes

and watermelons. With such innocence as this, he knew that he could spread it thick; and very soon after the preliminary details about his always having cherished a peculiar affection for this part of the country, and how General Lee had had no warmer admirer than himself, he was spreading it unmistakably thick. By the time he had informed them that it was not colonels and generals to whom he bowed the knee, but the enlisted man, the so-called common soldier, whose bleeding feet had blazed the trail for liberty with fearless shouts of triumph, Sergeant Jones was muttering to his neighbor, "How long more d'yu figure he'll slobber?" and the captain's mustache was standing out from his face like a shelf.

"That is what I am for!" perorated the wet-nurse. "I am for the enlisted man. The country looks to our beloved Purresident, but you look to me. Go forth, young men, for I am behind every one of you. No so-called military regulations shall insult your American manhood or grind you down while I stand sentinel at my post. If you are troubled, come to me and you shall have your rights. Go forth then, you who outshine their vaunted Cæsars, their licentious Alexanders, their pagan Plutos and

Aspasias! Go forth to be the bulwarks and imperishable heroes of our gullorious country!''

The watermelons cheered, the wet-nurse stepped down to let them shake his hand, and Captain Stone went home with his bride, in a speechless rage. He was able to speak presently.

"Still, Joshua," she mildly insisted, "young soldiers have so many sad temptations, I am glad he has their welfare at heart."

"Nonsense, Gwendolen," said the captain. "You'll soon know the army, and you'll see then that' such talk as his merely turns contented men into discontented babies."

"Nobody could ever be discontented with you, Joshua, I am sure," the bride, with sweet emotion murmured.

She was nineteen, the captain was forty-five and upon gazing at the rosy cheeks of his Gwendolen he would frequently assert that a man was always as young as he felt.

The Secretary, after inspecting the military post, dined with the mayor of the neighboring town. At this meal, when a cold bottle had been finished, the mayor went so far as to inquire: "Say, who was Aspasia?"

But the Secretary answered: "What a wonderful land is ours and what a beautiful city is yours."

II. The Energy Is Transmitted

The expectations of Sergeant Jones were entirely unfulfilled. Much experience in taking charge of recruits upon long railway journeys had taught him that their earnest faces were not always more stirring than the stars upon Old Glory; he knew that you do not invariably find that sort of face for thirteen dollars a month. He had generally been obliged to watch their purchases at way stations, he had not seldom been forced to remove bottles of strong spirits from their possession, and he had almost always found it necessary to teach some of them a lesson in obedience. Judge therefore of the sergeant's amazement when, after the first half day of journey, a long overgrown ruddy boy approached him and asked in unsoiled Southern accents: "Please, sah, can we sing?"

"Sing?" said Jones. "Sing what?"

" 'Pull foah the shoah, sailah.' We have learned to do it in parts back in our home."

"Yes," said Jones, "I guess you can sing that—in parts or as a whole."

"We sing it as a whole in parts, sah," explained the recruit with simplicity.

"Your name Anniston?" Jones inquired, abruptly suspicious.

"Bateau sah. Leonidas Bateau. My cousin, Xerxes Anniston, sits over yonder by the watah-coolah."

"Oh," said Jones.

"Yes, sah. Xerx he sings bass in our choir back in our home. Sistah Smith—"

"Who?" said the sergeant.

"Sistah Smith, sah, the wife of our ministah, Tullius C. Smith."

"Oh," said the sergeant.

"She is leadah of our choir back in our home. She is our best soprano, Sistah Mingory is our best alto, and Brother Macon Lafayette Young gets two notes lowah than any of our basses. He keeps the choicest grocery in town and is president of our Y. M. C. A. You'd ought to heard our quartet in the prayer from 'Moses in Egypt,' arranged by Sistah Mingory last Eastah Sunday."

The thoroughly good heart of Jones now warmed to this recruit. (I cannot hope that you will remember Jones. He was Specimen Jones long ago, before he joined the Army. Some of his doings are chronicled elsewhere.

He is an old member of the family.) "Made
Moses hum, did y'u?" said he. "I'll bet the
girls would sooner have a solo from you than
from Brother what's-his-name Lafayette."

"Sistah Smith," replied Leonidas, blush-
ing like the innocent watermelon that he was,
"did say that she couldn't see how they were
going to get along without my uppah regis-
tah."

Jones settled back in his seat. "Sing
away," said he.

Many songs were sung through Alabama
and Louisiana and Texas; virtuous songs
with no offending or even convivial word, and
none so frequently demanded by the passen-
gers as a solo from Leonidas,

How little do I love this vale of tears,

through which the chorus crooned a murmur-
ing accompaniment. West of San Antonio, they
played a game of riddles, and when Cousin
Xerxes (who seemed the wit of the party)
asked, "Why is Dass's solo like Texas? Because it's all in flats," and the recruits were
convulsed with merriment by this, Sergeant
Jones, listening to them in his seat behind,
muttered with compassion: "Their mothers
could hear every word they say." And friend-

liness was established between him and the recruits. They confided many things to him.

Yes; not a drop of vice's poison flowed in them, but at El Paso, while they waited, Leonidas, on saying to Jones, "What an elegant speech the Secretary of War gave us!" was astonished to hear the sergeant burst into strong language.

"That hypercrite!" exclaimed Jones. And the shocked Leonidas answered him.

And now began to fall the first chill upon their friendliness. The recruits were clean from vice, but the Secretary's poison was at work, the sugar of self-pity he had given them to swallow, the false sentiment over themselves, the sick notion they were objects of special sympathy, instead of stout young lads beginning life with about as many helps and hindrances as other stout young lads.

"Yes, he did say so!" declared Leonidas "Yes, he did, sah. He said he'd take care we was treated like gentlemen. He said he was behind us. And I guess he's the man to back up his word."

"Well," said Jones, making a final try, "I'll tell y'u." And he laid a hand on the young man's shoulder. "A man enlists to be a soldier—nothin' else. Not to be a gentleman, but just a soldier who obeys his orders—and nothin' else. I obey the captain, and he obeys the colonel, and he obeys the commanding general of the department, and so it goes clean to the top, and we're all soldiers obeyin' the President of the United States, and if bein' a gentleman consists in makin' things as pleasant and easy for others as y'u can, why, the chap in the army who obeys best is the best gentleman. There's remedies for injustice all right, but you keep thinkin' about your duties and you'll not need to think about your remedies. Understand?"

"Yes, sah," said Leonidas, without the faintest sign of comprehension. "But the Secretary is at the top and it's right in him to say the top should nevah forget to recognize the onaliable rights of the bottom. He said he was behind us."

"Oh, go sit down and give us some of your upper register!" cried Jones.

Thus did friendliness give place to estrangement. The watermelons laid their heads together and assured Leonidas that he had acted in a proper and spirited manner. In Sergeant Jones they confided no longer, for which he was man enough to lay the blame where it belonged. He handsomely cursed the Secretary of War, but what good did that do?

Arrived at Fort Chiricahua, the recruits fell into safe hands, though not perhaps entirely wise ones. The post chaplain was an earnest preacher of the same denomination as the Rev. Tullius C. Smith, and delighted to surround Leonidas and his band with the same customs and influences which they had known at home. They were soon known throughout the post as "The Shouters." This epithet came from their choir singing, which was no whit lessened by their new and not wholly religious environment. If Sergeant Jones or Captain Stone had looked for insubordination as a result of the Secretary's speech, it was an agreeable disappointment. The recruits were punctual, they were clean, they were assiduous at drill, they showed intelligence, they were model, both as youths and soldiers, and nothing kept them from a more than common popularity in their various troops unless it was that they were a little too model for the taste of the average enlisted man. The parade-ground was constantly melodious with their week-day practising for Sabbath exercises. Sister Smith had sent them much music from home, and the post learned to admire "Moses in Egypt" as arranged by Sister Mingory and interpreted by the upper register of Leonidas.

One person there was whom the strains of psalmody, as they floated from the open windows of the school-room, did not wholly please. Captain Stone disapproved of his Gwendolen's spending so much time alone with the melodeon and Leonidas. Almost as fittingly might a Senator's wife sing duets with her coachman, and all the ladies of the Post knew this—excepting Gwendolen! But he could not forbid her, at least not yet. Was she not his bride of scarce three months? In this new army world, where he had brought her so far from everything that she had always known, how could he deprive her of one great resource, he who had cut her off from so many? Time would steadily teach her the conduct suitable for an officer's wife, and then of her own accord she would put the proper distance between herself and the enlisted men.

"It is so unexpected, Joshua," she said once, "such an unexpected joy to be able to keep a good influence around those poor boys."

"What do you call them poor boys for?" inquired the captain.

"To come into so many temptations so far from home!" she exclaimed.

"They're not going to have you and the chaplain and the organ all their lives, Gwendolen."

"Now, Joshua, keep your mustache down! The Secretary of War—don't swear so dreadfully, darling! Don't!" And the bride stopped her lord's lips with her hand. "I won't mention him any more," she promised. "I must run now, or I'll be late for practising next Sunday's anthem with Leonidas Bateau."

Left on the porch of his quarters, the captain made the same remark about next Sunday's anthem that he had made about the Secretary of War; but Gwendolen, having departed, did not hear him, and soon from the open windows of the school-house floated the chords of the melodeon with a chorus led by Cousin Xerxes, and a solo on an upper register,

How little do I love this vale of teahs.

Would Gwendolen have been so eager to redeem some dried-up middle-aged sinner? I don't know. At any rate, in her solicitude for the spotless Leonidas, she was abreast with the advanced Philanthropy which holds prevention better than cure. Of course, not even to the most evil-minded could scandal arise from any of this. But when you see a wife of nineteen playing the organ for a trooper of twenty-two, and a husband of forty-five constantly remarking that a man is always as young as he feels, why, then you are at no great distance from comedy, and the joke draws nearer when the wife is anxious that the trooper should not feel the want of his mother, and the trooper retains the limpid innocence of the watermelon. The ladies of the Post tried to be indignant that an officer's wife should so much associate herself with enlisted men, but they could only laugh—and hush when the captain came by, and the men in barracks laughed—and hushed when the captain came by, and the poor captain knew it all. Meanwhile, the melodeon played on, the watermelons lifted their harmless hymns, and in the heart of Leonidas the Secretary's speech dwelled like honey but like gall in the heart of the captain. Had Captain Stone dreamed what sweet familiarity the hymns were breeding, he— but he did not dream, hence was his awakening all the more pronounced.

The day it came had made an ill beginning

with him. He had walked unexpectedly into
the kitchen before breakfast, and found there
his Chinaman putting a finishing crust on the
breakfast rolls. He had never been aware of
such a process. He had always particularly
enjoyed the crust. The Chinaman had just
reached the point where he withdrew the hot
rolls from the oven and sprayed them suddenly with cold water from his mouth. There
had ensued a dreadful time in the kitchen, and
no rolls for breakfast and no Chinaman for
dinner, and even as late as five o'clock the
captain's mustache had not completely flat-
tened down. Leonidas should have observed
this as he came up the captain's steps with a
message from the chaplain for the captain's
wife. They were waiting for her to come over
and play the melodeon for Sunday's anthem.

"Is Sistah Stone here?" Leonidas inquired.

"WHO?" said the captain, rising from his
chair, which fell backward with the movement.

"Is Sistah Stone here?" repeated Leonidas, mildly. "The chaplain says—"

You will meet the most conflicting accounts
of the spot where Leonidas first landed on
firm ground after leaving the captain's boot.
The colonel's orderly, who was standing in

front of the colonel's gate four houses farther
up the line, deposed that he "thought he
heard a something but didn't see what made
it." Mrs. Phillips declared she was sitting on
her porch two houses down the line, and "it
looked just like diving from a spring-board."
These were the only two disinterested witnesses. The afflicted Leonidas claimed that he
had gone from the porch clean over the front
gate, and Captain Stone said that he didn't
know and didn't care, but that if the gate
story was true, then he had projected one
hundred and sixty pounds forty measured
feet and felt younger than ever.

The version which Jones gave has (to me)
always seemed wholly satisfactory. "Don't
y'u go sittin' up nights over it," said Jones.
"Nobody'll never prove where he struck. But
what I seen was the captain come ragin' out
of his gate. He went over to the officers' club
and I knowed it was particular, for y'u could
have stood a vase of flowers on his muss-tash
without spillin' a drop. And next comes Leonidas a-flyin' by me, a-screechin', 'The Secretary shall hear of this!' And I seen the mark
on his pants and he tells me. 'Hard brushin'
will remove it,' I says to him, and he says,
'The Secretary shall hear of it!' And I says,

'Well, Leonidas, it sure ain't your upper
register that's damaged.' 'The Secretary,'
says he, but I got tired. 'If you was figuring
to be the captain's brother-in-law,' I says,
'you should have bruck it to him gently.' ''

III. The Vibrations Spread

And what did the afflicted Leonidas do now?
Sunday's anthem was dashed from his mind.
They waited for him, but he never came back,
nor was the melodeon again played by Sister
Stone. Leonidas, without waiting to brush off
anything, hastened to his own troop commander, told of the insult to American manhood and displayed the grievous traces upon
his trousers. When the captain found that he
was not demented, he meditated briefly and
spoke.

"Bateau, this is unfortunate, but it seems
to me out of military cognizance."

Leonidas mentioned the Secretary of War
for the third or fourth time, and asked permission to complain to the post commander.

"Think this over for a day," said his troop
commander, "and I'll see Captain Stone." On
the next day he resumed, "Captain Stone con-
firms every statement that you make, except
—er—the distance."

"It was ovah the gate," repeated Leonidas.
"But I would feel just the same if it was
not."

The troop commander was wise. "Very
well. You have my permission to make your
complaint."

Private Bateau stated his case in the Adjutant's office at Fort Chiricahua. The post
commander duly investigated the affair, and
Private Bateau was duly informed that his
complaint was deemed out of military cognizance. Private Bateau, thoroughly booked on
the machinery, now appealed to the Department Commander. He called in no clerk to
draft his grievance for him; with Cousin
Xerxes to help, he wrote:

"FORT CHIRICAHUA, A. T., Nov. 30, 188—.
"THE ADJUTANT-GENERAL, Department of
Arizona, Whipple Barracks, A. T. (Through
Military Channels.)

"*Sir.*—For the information of the commanding general of the department, I wish to
report Captain Joshua Stone of E Troop 4th
Cavalry for using brutal conduct toward me
at 5 p.m. 26th inst., at witch hour he insulted
me with his foot behaiving like no officer and
gentleman in a way I will not rite down. All

I did was bring word our choir was waiting
for Mrs. Stone to play like she always done
on the melodeum for church practiss wens-
day afternoons and saturday nights.''

''Very respectfully, your obedient servant,

''LEONIDAS BATEAU, Private,

Troop I, 4th Cav'y.''

This document Leonidas handed to the first
sergeant of his troop, who took it with the
daily morning report to the captain, who indorsed it, ''Respectfully forwarded to the
Adjutant-General, Department of Arizona
(through Post Commander). The facts in this
case are as follows,'' etc., and duly signed the
indorsement, and forwarded it the next day to
the Post Commander, who indorsed it, ''Respectfully forwarded to the Adjutant-General,
Department of Arizona, Whipple Barracks,
A. T. I find upon investigation,'' etc., ''and I
have cautioned Private Leonidas Bateau that
he ought to be more guarded in his language
when referring to an officer's wife, and I
recommend that no further action be taken
in this case.''

Do you perceive the wheels beginning to go
round? The letter of Leonidas, thus twice indorsed and signed by the captain of his troop

and the colonel commanding Fort Chiricahua, now flew forth and upward, directing its course duly to the headquarters of the Department of Arizona, and even while it was upon its way, a new song was heard among the enlisted men on all sides at the post. It was fitted to the tune of "Stables," its author was unknown, and it went something like this:

> SAY, have you seen my sister?
> I GUESS that I must have missed her,
> I'll SHOW you a handsome blister, etc.

It went something like that (sing it and you will see how glove-like it fits the tune), and it contributed nothing to the happiness of Leonidas; but it made him glad that nobody save Cousin Xerxes knew of the long, long letter which he had written to the Secretary of War and mailed outside the post.

And now the wheels began to turn at Whipple Barracks while Private Bateau was waiting for the Secretary of War to answer his private letter, and stand behind him. The Department Commander knew all about the Secretary of War; moreover, he was enlightened concerning this case by his favorite staff-officer, Lieutenant Jimmy St. Michael, of Kings Port, South Carolina. Jimmy received from

a brother lieutenant at Fort Chiricahua an
intimate and spirited account of the whole deplorable misadventure, describing Gwendolen
at length, and Captain Stone at length, and
the melodeon, and the choir practices, not
omitting a sketch of Leonidas and Cousin
Xerxes. This letter kept the young officers up
until past midnight, for Jimmy gave them a
choir practice upon his banjo, impersonating
now Sistah Stone and now Leonidas. But, as
I have said, the Commanding General of the
Department knew the Secretary of War and
therefore deemed a plentiful investigation into the affairs of Leonidas the wisest course.
He would not accept the views of the post
commander, as was his usual habit; there
must be an inspector. Now his Inspector-
General was off inspecting something at Fort
Apache; and so, that time should not be lost,
he summoned Jimmy St. Michael and directed
him to proceed to Fort Chiricahua. Jimmy
departed with a valise, a letter official to the
colonel, a message unofficial to the same officer, and his banjo, which he rarely left behind
him. With the solemnity proper to all inspec-
tors, he arrived upon the scene of the tragedy,
and not even the joy of the club could unbend
him. He was implored to give at least "But

he didn't saw the wood,'' that song which had
left a trail of gayety from Klamath and Bid-
well to Meade and San Carlos. Jimmy remained deaf to everything but duty. His slim
figure became every inch an inspector, his
neat hair was severe, his black eyes almost
funereal. He made many inquiries, he investigated everybody, and he seldom uttered any
longer comment than ''H'm, h'm!'' He knew
how rare it is for an inspector to say more
than this.

His old friends would have thought him engaged to be married or otherwise grievously
changed for the worse, had he not, on the
night his mission was ended, taken the cover
off his banjo. He gave the second entirely
original poem which the misfortunes of Leonidas had inspired. He sang it to a tune heard
in a popular play, and here it is:

Of War I am the popular Secretaree — O.
I am the popularest man in all the show.
There were one or two or three
More popular than me
Till I received my portofolee — O.

George Washington, they say, was popular long ago.
His name to-day is sometimes mentioned still, I know.
But where d'you think he'll be
If he's compared with me,
When I resign my portofolee — O?

The very day that I into the White House go
My friends shall see my gratitude is never slow;
And chief of all their clan
Shall be the enlisted man
For he shall have my portofolee — O!

Even Joshua smiled, and Joshua was a solemn man, not to speak of his delicate position regarding Leonidas. He sat up late, drank to the health of Jimmy St. Michael, and remarked that he doubted if Jimmy felt any younger than he did.

But the hour for poor Leonidas to smile had not yet come. There was silence most unaccountable from the Secretary of War, and the encouragement given by having an inspector come several hundred miles received presently a rude shock.

Jimmy St. Michael returned to Whipple Barracks and made a carefully solemn report to the Commanding General; but at the end of it, seeing that the Commanding General's solemnity was less careful, he ceased to be an inspector, and said with his engaging Kings Port accent:

"General, did you ever put sugar on a raw oyster and try to swallow it?"

"It can't be done!" declared the General. "I've known that since I was at the Military Academy."

"It can be done, sir, if you will pardon my contradicting you. I did it myself on a bet at the Military Academy."

"Good Lord!" said the General. "What was it like?"

"I realized, sir, that the combination does not belong in Nature's plan, any more than mixing politics with the United States Army."

"Ha, ha!" went the General. "Ha, ha! Not in Nature's plan!" And he proceeded to drop the necessary lemon-juice upon the Secretary's luckless raw oyster.

To poor Leonidas's original letter was now added a third duly dated indorsement: "Respectfully returned to the commanding officer, Fort Chiricahua, A. T. The Commanding General approves of your action in this case. The provoking speech of Priv't Leonidas Bateau, Troop I, 4th Cav'y, on the occasion of his visiting the quarters of his troop commander being considered sufficient grounds for the harsh treatment administered." This, with the signature of the Assistant Adjutant-General, arrived at Fort Chiricahua, and was followed by a fourth indorsement dated there and signed by the Post Adjutant: "Respectfully returned to the commanding officer,

Troop I, 4th Cav'y, inviting attention to the
2d and 3d indorsements hereon, the contents
of which will be communicated to Pvt. Leonidas Bateau, Troop I, 4th Cav. By order of,''
etc.

The wheels of redress had turned, all the
wheels, and ground out nothing. His troop
commander sent for Leonidas and read him
the indorsements. Leonidas, being instructed
by a "guard-house lawyer," demanded his
papers, which were delivered to him, as was
his right. These now went with his appeal to
Washington. For Leonidas had written home
to Sistah Smith, who had written to a Congressman, who had replied that he was ever
for justice. Thus, with a long new letter from
Leonidas to the Secretary of War (whose
silence still remained unaccountable), did official tidings of the outrage to American manhood at length, through the Adjutant General's Department, come to the man of the
"portofolee—O."

Buttons were pressed and clerks des-
patched with messages; and there ensued a
conference between the Congressman, the
Adjutant-General, the Secretary of War, and
the Lieutenant-General himself. The Congressman stated the case; the Secretary was

quite uneasy, and talked a great deal, taking care not to express a single idea; but the Lieutenant-General was quite easy and talked only thus much:

"Called her his sister? Got kicked? I should think so!"

"General, this is good in you to help us," said the Secretary, with symptoms of relief. "I did not wish to reach this conclusion without your corroboration."

Thus ended the conference. The original letter of Leonidas with its four indorsements pasted on it, and making quite a budget, now started its return course bearing a fifth indorsement containing the Secretary of War's opinion signed by one of the Assistant Adjutants-General. It travelled through the back channels that you know, passing Whipple Barracks and reaching the hungry, unsated Leonidas many weeks after all traces had vanished from his trousers. During these weeks his life had been made a sorry thing by that song about the blister. Not even the sympathy of Cousin Xerxes could sweeten his embittered days. They were wholesome for him, to be sure; they began to cure him of being a watermelon; they even gave him gradually a just estimate of the Secretary's speech at

McPherson, and he grew into a strapping young trooper with many of the trooper's habits in moderation. The only profane language that he used was in connection with the Secretary of War, whose tricky official language in his indorsement had utterly dodged his promise to stand behind him. But Leonidas could not comfortably live in a place where everybody remembered how he had (as Jones put it) "run around showing his pants." He took his discharge at the first opportunity, and became an eminent cow-boy in the neighborhood, with a man's full strength in his sinews, and a man's anger silent in his heart. The hour for him to smile had not yet come.

IV. The Energy Is Once Again Transmitted

You will doubtless have perceived the flaw in the Secretary's conduct before I can point it out to you. He should have written a letter to poor Leonidas with his own hand. It might not have been the easiest kind of letter for you or for me to compose; but for a statesman of the Secretary's ripeness it ought to have been the affair of five minutes. A few words of deep sympathy, a few words of hot indignation, a few words of sincere regret that he had not yet had time to remove all the obstructions which a despotic tradition set between him and the enlisted man—and, best of all, a few words of promise to see Leonidas on his coming tour through the Southwest—such a letter as this would have made Leonidas proud and happy, and comforted forever the tingling sensations that pierced him whenever he thought of his final choir practice. But as Leonidas seemed no longer of any possible use to the Secretary, the Secretary forgot all about him!

It was not understood at the ranch where Leonidas was now employed, why he so eagerly followed the printed chronicle of the Secretary's approach. Indeed, had you asked him to explain it himself, I doubt if he could have done so: the needle seeks the pole—but why? He would pore over the Tucson paper and learn how the Secretary had visited San Antonio and spoken to the soldiers there; how he had paused at El Paso, and spoken to the soldiers there; how he had visited Bayard, Bowie and Grant, and spoken at all three; and how he was expected on the train from Benson on the very next day, and would get off at Chiricahua station and drive to the post; how he would return thence and pro-

ceed to Lowell Barracks on his way to Yuma
and Los Angeles.

All this programme was of natural interest
to the officers and men at Fort Chiricahua,
but it seemed of unnatural interest to Leonidas. Concerning his absorption the other
cow-boys passed comments among themselves, but made none to him, because he had
altogether ceased to be a watermelon.

The smoke of a train in that country is to
be sighted from a great distance and for some
time before you can see the train, because the
smoke is very black and the train goes very
slowly. Also, the dust of a horseman or a
vehicle can be descried from afar. As the
smoke of the Secretary's train approached
the Chiricahua station, the dust of a seemly
military escort drew near from the direction
of the post, and the dust of a galloping cow-
boy came along the road from the ranch
where Leonidas was employed. By the platform of the station was assembled a little
group of citizens hoping for a speech; and by
the time the train made its deliberate arrival
complete, the escort was arrayed with due
military precision, the ambulance was at hand
near by, for the Secretary to step into when
he should feel ready, and a captain with two

lieutenants was preparing to salute the eminent statesman as he alighted from the car. He returned their greeting, and as he stepped forward to the end of the platform from which elevation he desired to say a few cordial and timely words to those waiting in the surrounding dust, the cow-boy entered the ticket office, but came out again on the platform, which was natural, since the ticket window was at the moment closed. The sight of the Secretary produced an immediate effect upon the appearance of the cow-boy. He seemed to grow larger.

"Friends and soldiers," said the Secretary, "I am always moved when I see an enlisted man—" and even with the words, he was moved conspicuously through the air and came down in the dust in a seated position. The leg of Leonidas had grown exceedingly muscular. Before anybody had regained his senses, the cow-boy was seen to dash away shouting on his horse across the railroad track, and pursuit did not overtake him. I am not sure if this was the fault of Captain Stone or Sergeant Jones, both of whom were in the chase.

It gravely damaged the Secretary's visit for him, but rendered it for many others a memorable success, especially for Captain Stone and Sergeant Jones. And Jones made so bold as to remark to Stone: "I think, if the captain pleases, that the Secretary won't never stand behind Leonidas like Leonidas has stood behind him."

"It is a great thing for a man to feel young," replied Captain Stone. His mustache was flat, smiling and serene.

Nobody knows whether or not the Secretary considered this mixing of politics and the army to be in Nature's plan.

IV

IT was a yellow poster, still wet with the rain. Against the wet, dark boards of the shed on which it was pasted, its color glared like a patch of flame.

A monstrous thunderstorm had left all space dumb and bruised, as it were, with the heavy blows of its noise. Outside the station in the washed, fresh air I sat waiting, staring idly at the poster. The damp seemed to make the yellow paper yellower, the black letters blacker. A dollar-sign, figures and zeros, exclamation points, and the two blackest words of all, *reward* and *murder,* were what stood out of the yellow. Reward and Murder had been printed big and could be seen far. Two feet away, on the same shed, was another poster, white, concerning some stallion, his place of residence, and the fee for his service. This also I had read, with equal inattention and idleness, but my eyes had been drawn to the yellow spot and held by it.

Not by its news; the news was now old,

since at every cabin and station dotted along
our lonely road the same poster had appeared. They had discussed it, and whether
he would be caught, and how much money he
had got from his victim. At Lost Soldier they
knew he had got ten thousand dollars, at Bull
Spring they knew he had got twenty, at
Crook's Gap it was more like twenty-five,
while at Sweetwater Bridge he had got nothing at all. What they did agree about was
that he would not be caught. Too much start.
Body hadn't been found on Owl Creek for a
good many weeks. Funny his friend hadn't
turned up. If they'd killed him, why wasn't
his body on Owl Creek too? If he'd got away,
why didn't he turn up? Such comments, with
many more, were they making at Lost Soldier,
Bull Spring, Crook's Gap, and Sweetwater
Bridge, and it was not the news on the poster
that drew my eye, but its mere yellow vibra-
tions. These in some way, caught my brain
in a net and held it still, so that thinking
stopped, and I was under a spell, torpid as
any plant or sponge—passive, perhaps, is the
truer word for my state.

When I was abruptly wakened from this
open-eyed sleep, I knew that I had been hearing a song for some time :—

> If that I was where I would be,
>   Then should I be where I am not;
> Here am I where I must be,
>   And where I would be I cannot.

It was the neigh of some horse in the stable, loud and sudden, that had burst the shell of my trance, causing thought to start to life again, as if with a leap; there I sat in the wagon, waiting for Scipio Le Moyne to come out of the house; there in my nostrils was the smell of the wet sage-brush and of the wet straw and manure, and there, against the gray sky, was an after-image of the yellow poster, square, huge, and blue. The smaller print was not reproduced, but Reward and Murder stood out clear, floating in the air. It moved with my eyes as I turned them to get rid of the annoying vision, and it at last slowly dissolved away over the head of the figure sitting on the corral with its back to me, the stock-tender of this stage station. It wore out as I listened to his song, and looked at him. He sang his song again, and I found that I now knew it by heart.

> If that I was where I would be,
>   Then should I be where I am not;
> Here am I where I must be,
>   And where I would be I cannot.

In the mountains, beyond the sage-brush, the thunderstorm was still splitting the dark cañons open with fierce strokes of light; the light seemed close, but it was a long time before its crashes and echoes came to us through the wet air. I could not see the figure's face, or that he moved. One boot was twisted between the bars of the corral to hold him steady, its trodden heel was worn to a slant; from one seat-pocket a soiled rag protruded, and through a hole below this a piece of his red shirt or drawers stuck out. A coat much too large for him hung from his neck rather than from his shoulders, and the damp, limp hat that he wore, with its spotted, unraveled hatband, somehow completed the suggestion that he was not alive at all, but had been tied together and stuffed and set out in joke. Certainly there were no birds here, or crops to frighten birds from; empty bottles were the only thing that man had sown the desert with at Rongis.[1] These lay everywhere. As the figure sat and repeated its song beneath the still wrecked and stricken sky, its back and its hat and its voice gave an impression of

[1] For reasons, those who in 188— named this place after its chief inhabitant, wished to disguise his name. This they accomplished by changing the order of the letters which spelled it.

loneliness, poignant and helpless. A windmill turned and turned and creaked near the corral, adding its note of forlornness to the song.

A man put his head out of the house. "Stop it," he said, and shut the door again.

The figure obediently climbed down and went over to the windmill, took hold of the rope hanging from its rudder, and turned the contrivance slowly out of the wind, until the wheel ceased revolving. I saw then that he was a boy.

The man put his head out of the house, this second time speaking louder: "I didn't say stop *that,* I said stop *it;* stop your damned singing." He withdrew his head immediately.

The boy—the mild, new yellow hair on his face was the unshaven growth of adolescence —stood a long while looking at the door in silence, with eyes and mouth expressing futile injury. Finally he thrust his hands into bunchy pockets and said:—

"I ain't no two-bit man."

He watched the door, as if daring it to deny this; then, as nothing happened, he slowly drew his hands from the bunchy pockets, climbed the corral at the spot nearest him, twisted the boot between the bars, and sat as before, only without singing.

The cloud and the thunder were farther away, but around us still, from unseen places, roofs and corners, dropped the leavings of the downpour. We faced each other, saying nothing; we had nothing to say. In the East we would have talked, but here in the Rocky Mountains an admirable habit of silence was generally observed under such conditions.

Thus we sat waiting, I for Scipio to come out of the house with the information he had gone in for, while the boy waited for nothing. *Waiting for nothing* was stamped plain upon him from head to foot, as it is stamped upon certain figures all the world over—figures seated in clubs, standing at corners, leaning against railroad stations and boxes of freight, staring out of windows. Those in the clubs die at last, and it is mentioned; the others of course die, too, only it is not mentioned. This boy's eyebrows were insufficient, and his front was as ragged as his back.

Presently the same man put his head out of the door. "You after sheep?"

I nodded.

"I could a-showed you sheep. Rams. Horns as big as your thigh—bigger'n *your* thigh. That was before tenderfeet came in and spoiled this country. Counted seven thousand.

on that there butte one morning before breakfast. Seven thousand and twenty-three, if you
want exact figgers. Set on this porch and
killed sheep whenever I wanted to. Some of
'em used to come on the roof. Counted eight
rams on the roof one morning before breakfast. Quit your staring!'' This was addressed to the boy on the corral. ''Why,
you're not a-going without another?'' This
convivial question was to Scipio, who now
came out of the house and across to me with
news of failure.

''I could a-showed you sheep—'' resumed
the man, but I was attending to Scipio.

''He don't know anything,'' said Scipio,
''nor any of 'em in there. But we haven't got
this country rounded up yet. He's just come
out of a week of snake fits, and, by the way it
looks, he'll enter on another about to-morrow
morning. But whisky can't stop *him* lying.''

''Bad weather,'' said the man, watching us
make ready to continue our long drive. ''Lots
o'lightning loose in the air right now. Kind o'
weather you're liable to see fire on the horns
of the stock some night.''

This sounded like such a promising inven-
tion that I encouraged him. ''We have nothing like that in the East.''

"H'm. Guess you've not. Guess you never seen sixteen thousand steers with a light at the end of every horn in the herd."

"Are they going to catch that man?" inquired Scipio, pointing to the yellow poster.

"Catch him? Them? No! But I could tell 'em where he's went. He's went to Idaho."

"Thought the '76 outfit had sold Auctioneer," Scipio continued conversationally.

"That stallion? No! But I could tell 'em they'd ought to." This was his good-by to us; he removed himself and his alcoholic omniscience into the house.

"Wait," I said to Scipio, as he got in and took the reins from me. "I'm going to deal some magic to you. Look at that poster. No, not the stallion, the yellow one. Keep looking at it hard." While he obeyed me I made solemn passes with my hands over his head. I kept it up, and the boy sat on the corral bars, watching stupidly. "Now look anywhere you please."

Scipio looked across the corral at the gray sky. A slight stiffening of his figure ensued, and he knit his brows. Then he rubbed a hand over his eyes and looked again.

"You after sheep?" It was the boy sitting on the corral. We paid him no attention.

"It's about gone," said Scipio, rubbing his eyes again. "Did you do that to me? Of course y'u didn't! What did?"

I adopted the manner of the professor who lectured on light to me when I was nineteen. "The eye being normal in structure and focus, the color of an after-image of the negative variety is complementary to that of the object causing it. If, for instance, a yellow disk (or lozenge in this case) be attentively observed, the yellow-perceiving elements of the retina become fatigued. Hence, when the mixed rays which constitute white light fall upon that portion of the retina which has thus been fatigued, the rays which produce the sensation of yellow will cause less effect than the other rays for which the eye has not been fatigued. Therefore, white light to an eye fatigued for yellow will appear blue—blue being yellow's complementary color. Shall I go on?"

"Don't y'u!" Scipio begged. "I'd sooner believe y'u done it to me."

"I can show you sheep." It was the boy again. We had not noticed him come from the corral to our wagon, by which he now stood. His eyes were now eagerly fixed upon me; as they looked into mine they seemed almost burning with some sort of appeal.

"Hello, Timberline!" said Scipio, not at all unkindly. "Still holding your job here? Well, you better stick to it. You're inclined to drift some."

He touched the horses, and we left the boy standing and looking after us, lonely and baffled. But when a joke was born in Scipio it must out:

"Say, Timberline," he called back, "better insure your clothes. Y'u couldn't replace 'em."

"I'm no two-bit man," retorted the boy with anger—that pitiful anger which feels a blow but cannot give one.

We drove away along the empty stage-road, with the mountains and the dying storm, in which a piece of setting sun would redly glow and vanish, making our leftward horizon, and to our right the great undulations of a world so large as to seem the universe itself. The air was wet still, and full of the wet sagebrush smell, and the ground was wet, but it could not be so long in this sandy region. Three hours would see us to the next house, unless we camped short of this upon Broke Axle Creek.

"Why Timberline?" I asked after several miles.

"Well, he came into this country the long,

lanky, innocent kid like you saw him, and he'd
always get too tall in the legs for his latest
pair of pants. They'd be half up to his knees.
So we called him that. Guess he's most forgot his real name.''

''What is his real name?''

''I've quite forgot.''

This much talk did for us for two or three
miles more.

''Must it be yellow?'' Scipio asked then.

''Red'll do it, too,'' I answered. ''Only you
see green then, I think. And there are
others.''

''H'm,'' observed Scipio. ''Most as queer
as chemistry. D' y'u know chemistry?''

''Why, what do you know?''

''Just the embalmin' side. Didn't y'u know
I assisted an undertaker wunst in Kansas
City?''

''What's that?'' I interrupted sharply, for
something out in the darkness had jumped.

''Does a stray deer scare you like that to-
night? Now, that embalmin' trick give me a
notion I'll work out some time. What do you
miss worst in camp grub?''

''Eggs,'' said I, immediately.

''That's you. Well, I'm going to invent embalmed eggs—somehow.''

"Hope you do," said I. "Do you believe I'm going to get sheep this time? It's all I came for."

"You'll get sheep," Scipio declared, "or I'll lose my job at Sunk Creek ranch." Judge Henry had lent him to me for my hunting trip. "Of course I'd not *call* 'em embalmed eggs," he finished.

"Condensed," I suggested. "Like the milk. Do you suppose the man really did go to Idaho?"

"They do go there—and they go everywheres else that's convenient—Canada, San Francisco, some Indian reservation. He'll never get found. I expect like as not he killed the confederate along with the victims—it's claimed there was a cook along, too. He's never showed up. It's a bad proposition to get tangled up with a murderer."

I sat thinking of this and that and the other.

"That was a superior lie about the lights on the steers' horns," I remarked next.

Scipio shoved one hand under his hat and scratched his head. "They say that's *so*," he said. "I've heard it. Never seen it. But—tell y'u—he ain't got brains enough to invent a thing like that. And he's too conceited to tell another man's lie."

"Well," I pondered, "there's Saint Elmo's fire. That's genuine."

"What kind of fire is that?"

"Mysterious lights that are seen at the ends of the yards and spars of ships. It's electricity. Often before a big storm, souls of dead sailor-men come back to warn the living, is what they say it is over in Brittany."

"Well, lightning scares me worse than ghosts."

He wouldn't listen when I attempted to speak of charged thunder clouds, and the positive, and the negative, and conductors, and Leyden jars. "That's a heap worse than the other stuff about yellow and blue," he objected. "Here's Broke Axle. D' y'u say camp here, or make it in to the station?"

"Well, if that filthy woman still keeps the station—"

"She does. We'll camp here. You'll get sheep," he now repeated in a voice of reassurance, and went his way to attend to the horses for the night.

The earth had dried, the plenteous stars were bright in the sky, we needed no tent over us, and merely spread my rubber blanket and the buffalo robes, and so beneath light covers waited for sleep to the gurgle, sluggish

and musical, of Broke Axle. Scipio's sleep
was superior to mine, coming sooner and
burying him deeper from the world of wake-
fulness. He did not become aware of a figure
sitting by our little fire of embers, whose
presence penetrated my thinner sleep until
my eyes opened and saw it. Such things give
me a shock, which, I suppose, must be fear,
but it is not at all fear of the mind. I lay
still, drawing my gun stealthily into a good
position and thinking what it were best to do;
but he must have heard me.

"Lemme me show you sheep."

"What's that?" It was Scipio starting to
life and action.

"Don't shoot Timberline," I said. "He's
come to show us sheep."

Scipio sat staring stupefied at the figure
by the embers, and then he slowly turned
his head round to me, and I thought he was
going to pour out one of those long, corrosive
streams of comment that usually burst from
him when he was enough surprised. But he
was too much surprised. "His name is
Henry Hall," he said to me very mildly.
"I've just remembered it."

The patient figure by the embers rose.
"There's sheep in the Washakie Needles.

Lots and lots and lots. I seen 'em myself in the spring. I can take you right to 'em. Don't make me go back and be stock-tender.'' He recited all this in a sort of rising wail until the last sentence in which the entreaty shook his voice.

''Washakie Needles is the nearest likely place,'' muttered Scipio.

''If you don't get any, you needn't to pay me any,'' urged the boy; and he stretched out an arm to mark his words and his prayer.

We sat in our beds and he stood waiting by the embers to hear his fate, while nothing made a sound but Broke Axle.

''Why not?'' I said. ''We were talking of a third man.''

''A man,'' said Scipio. ''Yes.''

''I can cook, I can pack, I can cook good bread, and I can show you sheep, and if I don't you needn't to pay me a cent,'' entreated the boy. There seemed something almost like anguish in his pleading.

''He sure means what he says,'' Scipio commented. ''It's your trip.''

Thus it was I came to hire Timberline.

Dawn showed him in the same miserable rags he wore on my first sight of him at the corral, and these proved his sole visible property of any kind; he didn't possess a change of anything, he hadn't brought away from Rongis so much as a handkerchief tied up with things inside it; most wonderful of all, he owned not even a horse—and in that country in those days five dollars' worth of horse was within the means of almost anybody.

But he was not unclean, as I had feared. He washed his one set of rags and his skin-and-bones body, by the light of the first sunrise on Broke Axle, and this proved a not too rare habit with him, which made all the more strange his neglect to throw the rags away and wear the new clothes I bought and gave him as we passed through Lander.

"Timberline," said Scipio the next day, "if Anthony Comstock came up in this country he'd jail you."

"Who's he?" screamed Timberline, sharply.

"He lives in Noo York, and he's agin the nood. That costume of yours is getting close on to what they claim Venus and other immoral Greek statuary used to wear."

After this Timberline put on the Lander clothes, but on one of his wash-days we discovered that he kept the rags next to his skin!

This clinging to such worthless things seemed probably the result of destitution, of having had nothing, day after day and month after month. His poor little pay at Rongis, which we gradually learned they had always got back from him by one trick or another, was less than half what I now gave him for his services, and I offered to advance him some of this at places where it could be spent; but he told me to keep it until he had earned the whole of it.

Yet he did not seem a miser; his willingness to help at anything in camp was unchanging, and a surer test of not being stingy was the indifference he showed to losing or winning the little sums we played at cards for after supper and before bed. The score I kept in my diary showed him to belong to the losing class. His help in camp was real, not merely well meant; the curious haze or blur in which his mind had seemed to be at the corral cleared away, and he was worth his wages. What he had said he could do, he did, and more. And yet, when I looked at him, he was somehow forever pitiful.

"Do you think anything is the matter with him?" I asked Scipio.

"Only just one thing. He'd oughtn't never to have been born."

"That probably applies to several million people all over this planet."

"Sure," assented Scipio cheerfully. He was not one of these.

" He's so eternally silent!" I said presently.

"A man don't ask to be born," pursued Scipio.

"Parents can't stop to think of that," I returned.

"H'm," mused Scipio. "Somebody or something has taken good care they'll never."

We continued along the trail, engrossed in our several thoughts, and I could hear Timberline behind us with the pack horses, singing:—

> If that I was where I would be,
> Then should I be where I am not.

Our mode of travel was changed at Fort Washakie. There we had left the wagon and put ourselves and our baggage upon horses, because we should presently be in a country where wagons could not go. I suppose that more advice is offered and less taken than of any other free commodity in the world. Before I had settled where to go for sheep, nobody could tell me where to go; now almost every one advised some other than the place

I had chosen. "Washakie Needles?" they
would repeat unfavorably; "Union Peak's
nearer"; or, "You go up Jakey's Fork"; or
"Red Creek's half as far, and twice as many
sheep"; or, "Last spring I seen a ram up
Dinwiddie big as a horse."

This discouragement, strung along our
road, had small weight with me because it
was just the idle talk of those dingy loafers
of the Western cabin and saloon who never
hunted, never did anything but sit still and
assume to know your own business better than
you knew it yourself; it was only once that the
vigorous words of some by-passer on a horse
caused Scipio and me to discuss dropping the
Washakie Needles in favor of the country at
the head of Green River. We were below Bull
Lake at the forking of the ways; none of us
had ever been in the Green River country,
while Timberline evidently knew the Washakie Needles well, and this was what finally
decided us. But Timberline had been thrown
into the strangest agitation by our uncer-
tainty. He had said nothing, but he walked
about, coming near, going away, sitting down,
getting up, instead of placidly watching his
fire and cooking; until at last I told him not
to worry, that wherever we went I should

keep him and pay him in any case. Then he spoke :—

"I didn't hire to go to Green River."

"What have you got against Green River?"

"I hired to go to the Washakie Needles."

His agitation left him immediately upon our turning our faces in that direction. What had so disturbed him we could not guess; but later that day Scipio rode up to me, bursting with a solution. He had visited a freighter's camp, a hundred yards off the road in the sage-brush (we were following the Embar trail), and the freighter, upon learning our destination, had said he supposed we were "after the reward." It did not get through my head at once, but when Scipio reminded me of the yellow poster and the murder, it got through fast enough: the body had been found on Owl Creek, and the middle fork of Owl Creek headed among the Washakie Needles. There might be another body,—the other Eastern man who had never been seen since,—and there was a possible third, the confederate, the cook; many held it was the murderer's best policy to destroy him as well.

Owl Creek had yielded no more bodies after that one first found. Perhaps the victims had

been killed separately. Before starting on
their last journey in this world, they had let
it get out somewhere down on the railroad
that they carried money; this was their awful
mistake, conducting death to them in the
shape of the man who had offered himself as
their guide, and whom they had engaged without more knowledge of him than he disclosed
to them himself. Red Dog was his name in
Colorado, where he was "wanted." The all-
day sitters and drinkers in the cabins along
the road had their omniscient word as to this
also: *they* could have told those Easterners
not to hire Red Dog!

So now we had Timberline accounted for
satisfactorily to ourselves; he was "after the
reward." We never said this to him, but we
worked out his steps from the start. As
stock-tender at Rongis he had seen that yellow
poster pasted up, and had read it, day after
day, with its promise of what to him was a
fortune. To Owl Creek he could not go alone,
having no money to buy a horse, and being
afraid, too, perhaps. If he could only find
that missing dead man—or the two of them—
he might find a clue. My sheep hunt had
dropped like a Providence into his hand.

We got across the hot country where rattlesnakes were thick, where neither man lived nor water ran, and came to the first lone habitation in this new part of the world—a new set of mountains, a new set of creeks. A man stood at the door watching us come.

"Know him?" I asked Scipio.

"I've heard of him," said Scipio. "He married a squaw."

We were now opposite the man's door. "You folks after the reward?" said he.

"After mountain sheep," I replied somewhat angry.

We camped some ten miles beyond him, and the next day crossed a low range, stopping near another cabin for noon. They gave us a quantity of berries they had picked, and we gave them some potatoes.

"After the reward?" said one of them as we rode away, and I contradicted him with temper.

"Lie to 'em," said Scipio. "Say yes." He developed his theory of truthfulness; it was not real falsehood to answer as you chose questions people had no right to ask; in fact, the only real lie was when you denied something wrong you had done. "And I've told hundreds of them, too," he concluded pensively.

Something had begun to weigh upon our cheerfulness in this new country. The reward dogged us, and we saw strange actions of people twice. We came upon some hot sulphur springs and camped near them, with a wide stream between us and another camp. Those people—two men and two women— emerged from their tent, surveyed us, nodded to us, and settled down again. Next morning they had vanished; we could see the gleam of empty bottles on the bank opposite where they had been. And once, riding out of a little valley, we sighted close to us through cottonwoods a horseman leading a pack horse out of the next little valley.

He did not nod to us, but pursued his parallel course some three hundred yards off, until a rise in the ground hid him for a while; when this was passed he was no longer where he should have been, abreast of us, but far to the front, galloping away. That was our last sight of him. We spoke of these actions a little. Did these people suspect us, or were they afraid we suspected them?

All we ever knew was that suspicion had now gradually been wafted through the whole air and filled it like a coming change of weather. I could no longer look at a rock or

a clump of trees without a disagreeable
thought: was something, or somebody, behind
the clump of trees and the rock? would
they come out or wait until we had passed?
This influence seemed to gather even more
thick and chill as we turned up the middle
fork of Owl Creek; magpies, that I had always liked to watch and listen to, had become
part of the general increasing uncomfortable-
ness, and their cries sounded no longer cheerful, but harsh and unfriendly.

As we rode up the narrowing cañon of Owl
Creek, the Washakie Needles, those twin
spires of naked rock, rose into view high
above the clustered mountain-tops, closing
the cañon in, shutting out the setting sun.
But the nearness of my goal and my sheep
hunt brought me no elation. Those miserable
questions about reward, the strange conduct
of those unknown people, dwelt in my mind.
I saw in memory the floating image of that
poster; I wondered if I, in my clambering for
sheep, should stumble upon signs—evidence
—an old camp—ashes—tent-pegs—or the
horrible objects that had come here alive and
never gone hence. I could not drive these
fancies from me amid the austere silence of
the place where *it* had happened.

"He *can* talk when he wants to."

It made me start, this remark of Scipio's as he rode behind me.

"What has Timberline been telling you?"

"Nothing. But he's been telling himself a heap of something." In the rear of our single-file party Timberline rode, and I could hear him rambling on in a rising and falling voice. He ceased once or twice while I listened, breaking out again as if there had been no interruption. It was a relief to have a practical trouble threatening us; if the boy was going off his head, we should have something real to deal with. But when I had chosen a camp and we were unsaddling and throwing the packs on the ground, Timberline was in his customary silence. After supper I walked off with Scipio where our horses were.

"Do you think he's sick?" I asked.

"I don't know," said Scipio. And that was all we said, for we liked the subject too little to pursue it.

Next morning I was over at the creek washing before breakfast. The sun was coming in through the open east end of our cañon, the shaking leaves of the quaking-asp twinkled in a blithe air, and a night's sleep had brought me back to a much robuster mood. I had my field-glasses with me, and far up, far up among patches of snow and green grass, I could see sheep on both sides of the valley.

"So you sleep well?" said Scipio.

"Like a log. You?"

"Like another. Somebody in camp didn't."

I turned and looked at Timberline cooking over at camp.

"Looking for the horses early this morning," pursued Scipio, "I found his tracks up and down all over everywheres."

"Perhaps he has found the reward."

Scipio laughed, and I laughed. It was the only thing to do. How much had the boy walked in the darkness?

"I think I'll take him with us," I then said. "I'd rather have him with us."

During breakfast we discussed which hill we should ascend, and, this decided on, I was about to tell Timberline his company was expected, when he saved me the trouble by requesting to be allowed to go himself. His usually pale, harmless eyes were full of some sort of glitter: did his fingers feel that they were about to clutch the reward?

The three of us left camp. It was warm summer in the valley by the streaming channel of our creek, and the quiet day smelled of the pines. We should not have taken horses, they served us so little in such a climb as that. On the level top our legs and breathing got relief, and far away up the next valley were sheep. This second top we reached, but they were gone to the next beyond, where we saw them across a mile or so of space. In the bottom below us ran the north fork of Owl Creek like a fine white wire drawn through the distant green of the pines. Up in this world peaks and knife-edged ridges bristled to our north away and away beyond sight.

We now made a new descent and ascent, but had no luck, and by three o'clock we stood upon a lofty, wet, slipping ledge that fell away on three sides, sheer or broken, to the summer and the warmth that lay thousands of feet below. Here it began to be very cold, and to the west the sky now clotted into advancing masses of thick thunder-cloud, black, weaving and merging heavily and swiftly in a fierce rising wind. We got away from this promontory to follow a sheep trail, and as we went along the backbone of the mountain, two or three valleys off to the right, long, black streamers let down from the cloud. They hung and wavered mistily close over the pines

that did not grow within a thousand feet of
our high level. I gazed at the streamers, and
discerned water, or something, pouring down
in them. Above our heads the day was still
serene, and we had a chance to make camp
without a wetting. This I suggested we
should do, since the day's promise of sport
had failed.

"No! no!" said Timberline, hoarsely.
"See there! We can get them. We're above
them. They don't see us!"

I saw no sheep where he pointed, but I saw
him. His eyes looked red-hot. He insisted the
sheep had merely moved behind a rock, and so
we went on. The strip of clear sky narrowed,
and gray bars of rain were falling between us
and the pieces of woodland that, but a moment since, had been unblurred. Blasts of
frozen wind rose about us, causing me to put
on my rubber coat before my fingers should
grow too numb to button it. We moved forward to a junction of the knife-ridges upon
which a second storm was hastening from the
southwest over deep valleys that we turned
our backs upon, and kept slowly urging our
horses near the Great Washakie Needle.

We stopped at the base of its top pinnacle,
glad to reach this slanting platform of

comparative safety. No sheep were anywhere, but I had ceased to care about sheep. Jutting stones, all but their upturned points and edges buried in the ground, made this platform a rough place to pick one's way over—but this was a trifle. From these jutting points a humming sound now began to rise, a sort of droning, which at first ran about here and there among them, with a flickering, æolian capriciousness, then settled down to a steady chord: the influence of the electric storm had encircled us. We all looked at each other, but turned immediately again to watch the portentous, sublime scene.

At the edge of our platform the world fell straight a thousand feet down to a valley like the bottom of a cauldron; on the far side of the cauldron the air, like a stroke of magic, became thick white, and through it leaped the first lightning, a blinding violet. An arm of the storm reached over to us, the cauldron sank from sight in a white sea, and the hail cut my face so that I bowed it down. Mixed with the hail fell softer flakes, which, as they touched the earth glowed for a moment like tiny bulbs, and went out. On the ground I saw what looked like a tangle of old, human footprints in the hard-crusted mud, which the pellets of the swarming hail soon filled. This tempest of flying ice struck my body, my horse, raced over the ground like spray on the crest of breaking waves, and drove me to dismount and sit under the horse, huddled together even as he was huddled against the fury and the biting pain of the hail.

From under the horse's belly I looked out upon a chaos of shooting, hissing white, through which, in every direction, lightning flashed and leaped, while the fearful crashes behind the curtain of the hail sounded as if I should see a destroyed world when the curtain lifted. The place was so flooded with electricity that I gave up the shelter of my horse, left my rifle on the ground and moved away from the vicinity of these points of attraction. Of my companions I had not thought; I now noticed them, crouching separately, much as I crouched.

So I sat in the stinging hail—I know not how long—chilled from spine to brisket, my stiff boots growing wet, my hat a pulp like my discarded gloves, the melted hail trickling from the rubber coat to my legs. At length the hail-stones fell more gently, the near view opened, revealing white winter on all save the steep, gray Needles; the thick, white curtain

of hail departed slowly; the hail where I was
fell more scantily still.

It was slowly going away,—the great low-
prowling cloud,—we should presently be left
in peace unscathed, though it was at its tricks
still. Its brimming, spilling-over electricity
was now playing a new prank—mocking my
ears with crackling noises, as of a camp-fire
somewhere on earth, or in air. While I
listened curiously to these, my eye fell
on Timberline. He was turning, leaning,
crouching, listening, too. When he crouched, it
was to peer at those old footprints I had noticed. There was something frightful in the
sight of his face, shrunk to half its size, and
I called to reassure him, and beckoned that
it was all right, that we were all right. I
doubt if he saw or heard me.

Something somewhere near my head set up
a delicate sound. It seemed in my hat. I rose
and began to wander, bewildered by this. The
hail was now falling very fine and gentle,
when suddenly I was aware of its stinging
behind my ear more sharply than it had done
at all. I turned my face in its direction and
found its blows harmless, while the stinging
in my ear grew sharper. The hissing continued close to my head whenever I walked.

It resembled the little watery escape of gas from a charged bottle whose cork is being slowly drawn.

I was now more really disturbed than I had been during the storm's worst, and meeting Scipio, who was also wandering, I asked if he felt anything. He nodded uneasily, when, suddenly, I snatched off my hat. The hissing was in the brim, and it died out as I looked at the leather and the stitches. I expected to see some insect there, or some visible reason for the noise. I saw nothing, but the pricking behind my ear had also stopped. Then I knew my wet hat had been charged like a Leyden jar with electricity. Scipio, who had watched me, jerked his hat off also.

"Lights on steer horns are nothing to this," I began, when a piercing scream cut me short.

Timberline, at the other side of the stony platform, had clapped his hands to his head.

"Take off your hat," I shouted.

But he had fallen on his knees, and was ripping, tearing his clothes. He plucked and dragged at the old rags next his skin. Then he flung his hands to the sky.

"O God!" he screamed. "Oh, Jesus! Keep him off me! Oh, save me!" His glaring face now seemed fixed on something close to him. "Leave me go! I didn't push you over. You know he made me push you. I meant nothing. I knowed nothing, I was only the cook. Why, I liked you—you was kind to me. Oh, why did I ever go! There! Take it back! There's your money! He give it to me when you was dead to make me hush up. There! I never spent a cent of it!"

He tore from his rags the hush-money that had been sewed in them, and scattered the fluttering bills in the air. Then once more he clapped his hands to his head as he kneeled.

"Take off your hat!" I cried again.

He rose, stared wildly, and screamed: "I tell you you've got it all. It's all he gave to me!"

The next moment he plunged into the cauldron, a thousand feet below.

On the following day we found the two bodies—that second victim the country had wondered about, and the boy. And we counted the money, the guilty money that had for a while closed the boy's innocent mouth: five ten-dollar bills! Not much to hide murder for, not much to draw a tortured soul back to the scene of another's crime.

V

THE GIFT HORSE

HIGH up the mountain amid white Winter I sat, and looked far down where still the yellow Autumn stayed, looked at Wind River shrunk to map-size, a basking valley, a drowsy country, tawny and warm, winding southeastward away to the tawny plain, and there dissolving with air and earth in one deep, hazy, golden sleep. Somewhere in that slumberous haze beyond the buttes and utmost foothills, burrowed into the vast unfeatured level, lay my problem, Still Hunt Spring.

I had inquired much about Still Hunt Spring. Every man seemed to know of it, but no man you talked with had been to it. Description of it always came to me at second hand. Scipio I except; Scipio assured me he had once been there. It was no easy spot to find; a man might pass it close and come back and pass it on the other side, yet never know it was at his elbow: so they said. The Indians believed a supernatural thing about it—that it was not there every day, and few of them

129

would talk readily about it; yet it was they who had first showed it to the white man. And because they repeated concerning a valley two hundred feet deep, a mile long, and a quarter-mile wide at its widest, this haunted legend of presence and absence, its name now possessed my mind. Like a strain of music it recurred to my thoughts each day of my November hunting in the mountains of Wind River. Still Hunt Spring; down there, somewhere in that drowsy distance, it lay. One trail alone led into it; from one end of the secret ravine to the other—they said—grew a single file of trees lank and tall as if they stood on stilts to see out over the top, and at the further end was a spring, small, cold, and sweet. Though it welled up in the midst of sage-brush desert, there was no alkali—they said—in that water. Still Hunt Spring!

That night I announced to my two camp companions my new project: next summer I should see Still Hunt Spring for myself.

"Alone?" Scipio inquired.

"Not if you will come."

"It is no tenderfoot's trail."

"Then if I find it I shall cease to be a tenderfoot."

"Go on," said Scipio, with indulgence. "We'll not let you stay lost."

"It is no tenderfoot's place," the cook now muttered.

"Then you have been there?" I asked him.

He shook his head. "I am in this country for my health," he drawled. On this a certain look passed between my companions, and a certain laugh. A sudden suspicion came to me, which I kept to myself until next afternoon when we had broken this camp where no game save health seemed plentiful, and were down the mountains at Horse Creek and Wind River.

"I don't believe there is any such place as Still Hunt Spring."

This I said sitting with a company in the cabin known later on the Postal Route map as Dubois. The nearest post-office then was seventy-five miles away. No one spoke until a minute after, I suppose, when a man slowly remarked: "Some call that place Blind Spring."

He was presently followed by another, speaking equally slowly: "I've heard it called Arapaho Spring."

"Still Hunt Spring is right." This was a heavy, rosy-faced man of hearty and capable appearance. His clothes were strong and good, made of whipcord, but his maroon-colored straw hat so late in the season was

the noticeable point in his dress. His voice
was assertive, having in it something of au-
thority, if not of menace. "Some claim
there's such a place," he continued, eyeing
me steadily and curiously, "and some claim
there's not." Here he made a pause. "But
I tell you there is."

He still held his eye upon me with no
friendliness. Were they all merely playing on
my tenderfoot credulity, or what was it? I
was framing a retort when sounds of trouble
came from outside.

"Man down in the corral," exclaimed somebody. "It's that wild horse."

Scipio met us, running. "No doctor here?"
he panted. "McDonough has bruck his leg,
looks like."

But the doctor was seventy-five miles away
—like the post-office.

"Who's McDonough?" inquired the rosy-
faced man with the straw hat.

A young fellow from Colorado, they told
him, a new settler on Wind River this summer. He had taken up a ranch on North Fork
and built him a cabin. Hard luck if he had
broken his leg; he had a bunch of horses; was
going to raise horses; he had good horses.
Hard luck!

We found young McDonough lying in the corral, propped against a neighbor's kindly knee. The wild horse was snorting and showing us red nostrils and white eyes in a far corner; he had reared and fallen backward while being roped, and the bars had prevented dodging in time. Dirt was ground into McDonough's flaxen hair, the skin was tight on his cheeks, and his lips were as white as his large, thick nails; but he smiled at us, and his strange blue eyes twinkled with the full spark of undaunted humor.

"Ain't I a son-of-a-bitch?" he began, and shook his head over himself and his clumsiness. Further speech was stopped by violent retching, and I was enough of a doctor to fear that this augured a worse hurt than a broken leg. But no blood came up, and he was soon talking to us again, applying to himself sundry jocular epithets which were very well in that rough corral, but must stay there.

He was lifted to the only bed in the cabin, no sound escaping him, though his lips remained white, and when he thought himself unobserved he shut his eyes; but kept them open and twinkling at any one's approach. They were strange, perplexed eyes, evidently large, but deep-set, their lids screwed together; later that evening I noticed that he held his playing-cards close to them, and slightly to one side. Scipio called him "skewbald," but I could see no such defect. He was not injured internally, it proved later, but his right leg was broken above the ankle. We had to cut his boot off, so swollen already was the limb. The heavy man with the straw hat advised getting him to the hospital at the post without delay, and regretted he himself had not come up the river in his wagon; he could have given the patient a lift. With this he departed upon a tall roan horse, with an air about him of business and dispatch uncommon in these parts. Wind River horsemen mostly looked and acted as if there was no such thing as being behind time, there being no such thing as time.

"Who is he?" I asked, looking after the broad back of whipcord and the unseasonable straw hat.

All were surprised. What? Not know Lem Speed? Biggest cattleman in the country. Store and a bank in Lander. House in Salt Lake. Wife in Los Angeles. Son at Yale.

"Up here looking after his interests?" I pursued.

"Up here looking after his interests." My

exact words were repeated in that particular tone which showed I was again left out of something.

"What's the matter with my questions?" I asked.

"What's the matter with our answers?" said a man. Truly, mine had been a tenderfoot speech, and I sat silent.

McDonough's white lips regained no color that night, and the skin drew tighter over the bones of his face as the hours wore on. He was proof against complaining, but no stoic endurance could hide such pain as he was in. Beneath the sunburn on his thick hand the flesh was blanched, yet never did he once ask if the hay wagon was not come for him. They had expected to get him off in it by seven, but it did not arrive until ten minutes before midnight; they had found it fifteen miles up the river, instead of two. Sitting up, twisted uncomfortably, he played cards until one of the company, with that lovable tact of the frontier, took the cards from him, remarking, "You'll lose all you've got," and, with his consent, played his hand and made bets for him. McDonough then sank flat, watching the game with his perplexed, half-shut eyes.

What I could do for him I did; it was but

little. Finding his leg burning and his hand cold, I got my brandy—their whisky was too doubtful—and laid wet rags on the leg, keeping them wet. He accepted my offices and my brandy without a sign; this was like most of them, and did not mean that he was not grateful, but only that he knew no way to say so. Laudanum alone among my few drugs seemed applicable, and he took twenty drops with dumb acquiescence, but it brought him neither sleep nor doze. More I was afraid in my ignorance to give him, and so he bore, unpalliated, what must have become well-nigh agony by midnight, when we lifted him into the wagon. So useless had I been, and his screwed-up eyes, with their valiant sparkle, and his stoic restraint, made me feel so sorry for him, that while they were making his travelling bed as soft as they could I scrawled a message to the army surgeon at the Post. "Do everything you can for him," I wrote, "and as I doubt if he has five dollars to his name, hold me responsible." This I gave McDonough without telling him its contents. Off they drove him in the cold, mute night; I could hear the heavy jolts of the wagon a long way. Six rock fords lay between here and Washakie, and Scipio thus summed up

the seventy-five miles the patient had before
him: "I don't expect he'll improve any on
the road."

In new camps among other mountains I
now tried my luck through deeper snow,
thicker ice, and colder days, coming out at
length lean and limber, and ravenous for
every good that flesh is heir to, yet reluctant
to turn eastward to that city life which would
unfailingly tarnish the bright, hard steel of
health. Of Still Hunt Spring I spoke no more,
but thought often, and with undiscouraged
plans to visit it. I mentioned it but once again.
Old Washakie, chief of the Shoshone tribe,
did me the honor to dine with me at the military post which bore his name. Words cannot
describe the face and presence of that old
man; ragged clothes abated nothing of his
dignity. A past like the world's beginning
looked from his eyes; his jaw and long white
hair made you silent as tall mountains make
you silent. After we had dined and I had
made him presents, he drew pictures in the
sand for me with his finger. Not as I expected,
almost to my disappointment, this Indian betrayed no mystery concerning the object of
my quest.

"Hé!" he said (it was like a shrug). "No

hard find. You want see him? Water pretty good, yes. Trees heap big. You make ranch maybe?''

When he heard my desire was merely to see Still Hunt Spring, I am not certain he understood me, or if so, believed me. ''Hé!'' he exclaimed again, and laughed because I laughed. ''You go this way,'' he said, beginning to trace a groove in the sand. ''So.'' He laid a match here and there and pinched up little hillocks, and presently he had it all set forth. I tore off a piece of wrapping-paper from the stove and copied the map carefully, with his comments. The place was less distant than I had thought. I thanked him, spoke of returning ''after one snow'' to see him and Still Hunt Spring. ''Hé!'' he shrugged. Then he mounted his pony, and rode off without any ''good-by,'' Indian fashion. I counted it a treasure I had got from him.

McDonough's leg had knit well, and I met him on crutches crossing the parade ground. He was discharged from hospital, and (I will not deny it) his mere nod of greeting seemed somewhat too scant acknowledgment of the good will I had certainly tried to show him. Yet his smile was very pleasant, and while I noted his face, no longer embrowned with sun and riding, but pale from confinement, I noted also the unsubdued twinkle in his perplexed eyes. After all, why should I need thanks? As he hobbled away with his yellow hair sticking out in a cowlick under his hat behind, I smiled at my own smallness, and wished him good luck heartily.

The doctor, whose hospitable acquaintance I had made on first coming through the Post this year, would not listen to my paying him anything for his services to McDonough. Army surgeons were expected, he said, to render what aid they could to civilians, as well as to soldiers, in the hospital; he good-humoredly forbade all the remonstrance I attempted. When civilians could pay him themselves, he let them do so according to their means; it was just as well that the surrounding country should not grow accustomed to treating "Uncle Sam" as a purely charitable institution. McDonough had offered to pay, when he could, what he could afford. The doctor had thought it due to me to let him know the contents of my note, and that no such arrangement could be allowed.

"And what said he to that?" I asked.

"Nothing, as usual."

"Disgusted, perhaps?"

"Not in the least. His myopic eyes were just as cheerful then as they were the second before he fainted away under my surgical attentions. He scorned ether."

"Poor fellow! He's a good fellow!" I exclaimed.

"M'm," went the doctor, doubtfully.

"Know anything against him?" I asked.

"Know his kind. All the way from Assiniboine to Lowell Barracks."

"It has made you hard to please," I declared.

"M'm," went the doctor again.

"Think he'll not pay you?"

"May. May not."

"Well, good-by, Cynic."

"Good-by, Tenderfoot."

The next morning, had there been time to catch the doctor, I could have proved to him that he was hard to please. At the moment of my stepping into the early stage I had a surprise. McDonough had been at breakfast at the hotel, and had said nothing to me; a nod sufficed him, as usual—it was as much social intercourse as was customary at breakfast, or, indeed, at any of the meals. The stage rattled up as I sat, and I, its only passenger, rose and spoke a farewell syllable to Mc-

Donough, who repeated his curt nod. My next few minutes were spent in paying the bill, seeing my baggage roped on behind the stage, and in bidding Scipio good-by. One foot was up to get into the vehicle when a voice behind said, "So you're going."

There was McDonough, hobbled out after me to the fence. He stood awkwardly at the open gate, smiling his pleasant smile. I replied yes, and still he stood.

"Coming next year?"

Again I said yes, and again he stood silent, smiling and awkward. Then it was uttered; the difficult word which shyness had choked: "If you come, you shall have the best horse on the river."

Before I could answer he was hobbling back to the hotel. His untrained lips had at last spoken from his heart.

I drove away, triumphing over the doctor, and in my thoughts my holiday passed in review,—my camps, and Scipio, and Still Hunt Spring, and most of all this fellow with his broken leg and perplexed eyes—perplexed at life in general, I should think.

At Lander, they said, had I come two days earlier, I should have had the company of Lem Speed. So he and his maroon straw hat

came into my thoughts, too. He had started
for California, I heard from the driver, whose
society I sought on the box. He assured me
that Lem Speed was rich, but that I carried
better whisky. Trouble was "due" in this
country, he said (after more of my whisky),
"pretty near" the sort of trouble they were
having on Powder River. For his part he did
not wonder that poor men got tired of rich
men; not that he objected to riches, but only
to hogs. He had nothing against Lem Speed.
Temptation to steal stock had never come his
way, but he could understand how poor men
might get tired of the big cattlemen—some
poor men, anyhow. Yes, trouble was "sure
due"; what brought Lem Speed up here so
long after the beef round-up? Still, he
"guessed" he hadn't told Lem Speed anything that would hurt a poor fellow. Lem
Speed had "claimed" he was up here about
his bank. If so, why had he gone up Wind
River, and all around Big Muddy, and over to
the Embar? The bank was not there. No, sir;
the big cattlemen were going to "demon-
strate" over here as they had on the Dry
Cheyenne and Box Elder. I perceived
"demonstration" to be the driver's word for
the sudden hanging of somebody without due

process of law, and I expressed a doubt as to
its being needed here; I had heard nothing of
cattle or horses being stolen. This he received
in silence, presently repeating that Lem
Speed hadn't got anything from *him*. We
broke off this subject for mines, and after
mines we touched on topic after topic, until I
confided to him the story of McDonough.

"Of course I would never accept the
horse," I finished.

"Why not?"

"Well—well—it would hardly be suitable."

"Please yourself," said the driver, curtly,
and looking away. "Such treatment would
not please me."

"You mean, 'never look a gift horse in the
mouth,' as we say?"

"I don't know as I ever said that." A steep
gulley in the road obliged him to put on the
brake and release it before he continued: "I'd
not consider I had the right to do a man a
good turn if I wasn't willing for him to do *me*
one."

"But I really did nothing for him."

"Please yourself. Maybe folks are different East."

"Well," I ended, laughing, "I understand
you, and am not the hopeless snob I sound

like, and I'll take his horse next summer if you will take a drink now.''

We finished our journey in amity.

The intervening months, whatever drafts they made upon my Rocky Mountain health, weakened my designs not a whit; late June found me again in the stagecoach, taking with eagerness that drive of thirty-two jolting hours. Roped behind were my camp belongings, and treasured in my pocket was Chief Washakie's trail to Still Hunt Spring. My friend, the driver, was on the down stage; and so, to my regret, we could not resume our talk where we had left it; but I again encountered at once that atmosphere of hinted doings and misdoings which had encompassed me as I went out of the country. At the station called Crook's Gap I came upon new rumors of Lem Speed, and asked, had he come about his bank again?

"You and him acquainted?" inquired a man on a horse. And, on my answering that I was not, he cursed Lem Speed slow and long, looking about for contradiction; then, as none present took it up, he rode sullenly away, leaving silence behind him.

When I alighted next afternoon at the Washakie post-trader's store and walked back

to the private office of the building whither
I was wont always to repair, what I saw in
that private room, through a sort of lattice
which screened it off from the general public,
was a close-drawn knot of men round a table,
and on a chair a maroon-colored straw hat!
Rather hastily the post-trader came out, and,
shaking my hand warmly, drew me away from
the lattice. After a few cordial questions he
said: ''Come back this evening.''

"Does he never get a new hat?" I asked.

"Hat? Who? What? Oh; yes, to be
sure!" laughed the post-trader. "I'll tell him
he ought to.''

I sought out the doctor, soon learning from
him that McDonough had paid him for his
services. But this had not softened his opinion
of the young fellow, though he had heard
nothing against him, nor even any mention of
his name; he repeated his formula that he had
known McDonough's kind all the way from
Assiniboine to Lowell Barracks, whereupon
I again called him "cynic," and he retorted
with "tenderfoot," and thus amicably I left
him for my postponed gossip with the post-
trader. I found him hospitable, but preoccu-
pied, holding a long cigar unlighted between
his taciturn lips. Each topic that I started

soon died away: my Eastern news; my summer plans to ramble with Scipio across the Divide on Gros Ventre and Snake; the proposed extension of the Yellowstone Park—everything failed.

"That was quite a company you had this afternoon," I said, reaching the end of my resources.

"Yes. Nice gentlemen. Yes." And he rolled the long, unlighted cigar between his lips.

"Cattlemen, I suppose?"

"Cattlemen. Yes."

"Business all right, I hope?"

"Well, no worse than usual."

Here again we came to an end, and I rose to go.

"Seen your friend McDonough yet?" said he, still sitting.

"Why, how do you know he's a friend of mine?"

"Says so every time he comes into the Post."

"Well, the doctor's all wrong about him!" I exclaimed, and gave my views. The post-trader watched me in his tilted chair, with a half-whimsical smile, rolling his eternal cigar, and I finished with the story of the horse.

Then the smile left his face. He got up slowly, and slowly took a number of turns round his office, pottered with some papers on his desk, and finally looked at me again.

"Tell me if he does," he said.

"Offer the horse? I shall not remind him— and I should take it only as a loan."

"You tell me if he does," repeated the post-trader, now smiling again, and so we parted.

"I wonder what he didn't say?" I thought as I proceeded to the hotel; for he had plainly pondered some remarks and decided upon silence. Between them, he and the doctor had driven me to a strong hope that McDonough would vindicate my opinion of him by making good his word. At breakfast next morning at the hotel one of the invariable characters at such breakfasts, an unshaven person in tattered overalls, with rope-scarred fists and grimy knuckles, to me unknown, asked:—

"Figure on meeting your friend McDonough?"

"Not if he doesn't figure on meeting me."

They all took quiet turns at looking at me until some one remarked:—

"He ain't been in town lately."

"I'm glad his leg's all right," I said.

"Oh, his leg's all right."

The tone of this caused me to look at them. "Well, I hope he's *all* all-right!"

Not immediately came the answer: "By latest reports he was enjoying good health."

Truly they were a hopeless people to get anything direct from. Indirectness is by some falsely supposed to be a property of only the highly civilized; but these latter merely put a brighter and harder polish on it.

That afternoon I drove with my camp things out of town in a "buggy,"—very different from the Eastern vehicle which bears this name,—and the next afternoon between Dinwiddie and Red Creek, on a waste stretch high above the river, who should join me but Mc-Donough. He was riding down the mountain apparently from nowhere, and my pleasure at seeing him was keen. His words were few and halting, as they had been the year before, and in his pleasant, round face the blue eyes twinkled, screwed up and as perplexed as ever. I abstained from more than glancing at the fine sorrel that he rode, lest I should seem to be hinting.

"Water pretty low for this season," he said.

"Was there not much snow?"

"Next to none, and went early."

I turned from my direct course and camped at his cabin on North Fork.

"What's your hurry?" he said next morning, when I was preparing to go.

There was no hurry; those days had no hurry in them, and I bless their memory for it. I sat on a stump, smoking a "Missouri meerschaum," and unfolding to him my plans. To the geography of my route he listened intently—very intently.

"So you're going to keep over the other side the mountains?" he said.

"Even to Idaho," I answered, "and home that way."

"Not back this way?"

"Not this year."

He thought a little while. "You're settled as to that?"

"Quite."

He rose, and put some wood into the stove in his cabin; then he returned to me where I sat on the stump. "Sure you're quite settled you'll keep on the west side of the Divide?"

"Goodness!" I laughed, "why should I lie to you?"

Again he pondered in silence, and I could

not imagine what he had in his mind. What had my being east or being west of the mountains to do with him?

He now jerked his head toward the corral. "Like him?" he inquired gruffly. It was the sorrel horse that he meant, and I perceived that it was standing saddled. I said nothing. The fellow's embarrassment embarrassed me. "Like him?" he repeated.

"Looks good to me," I replied, adopting his gruffness.

He rose and brought the horse to me. "Get on."

"Hulloa! You've got my saddle on him."

"Get on. He ain't the one that bruck my leg."

I obeyed. Thus was the gift offered and accepted. I rode the horse down and up the level river bottom. "How shall I get him back to you?" I asked.

McDonough's face fell. "He'll be all right in the East," he protested.

I smiled. "No, my good friend. Not that. Let me send him back with the outfit."

We compromised on this, and caught trout for the rest of the day, also shooting some young sage chickens. The sorrel proved a fine animal. Again McDonough delayed my departure. "I can broil those chickens fine," he said, "and—and you'll not be back this way."

He would not look at me as he said this, but busied himself with the fire. He was lonely, and liked my company, and couldn't say so. Dense doctor! I reflected, not to have been warmed by this nature. But later this friendless fellow touched my heart more acutely. A fine thought had come to me during the evening: to leave my wagon here, to leave a note for Scipio at the E-A outfit, to descend Wind River to the Sand Gulch, strike Washakie's trail to the northeast of Crow Heart Butte, and on my vigorous sorrel find Still Hunt Spring by myself. The whole ride need take but two days. I think I must have swelled with pride at the prospect of this secret achievement, to be divulged, when accomplished, to the admiring dwellers on Wind River. But I intended to have the pleasure of divulging it to McDonough at once, and I forthwith composed a jeering note to Scipio Le Moyne.

"Esteemed friend" (this would anger him immediately); "come and find me at Still Hunt Spring, if you don't fear getting lost. If you do, avoid the risk, and I will tell you all about it Friday evening. Yours, Tenderfoot."

I pushed this over to McDonough, who was practising various cuts with a pack of cards. "That will make Scipio jump," I said.

Somewhat to my disappointment, it did not have this or any effect upon McDonough. He held the paper close to his eyes, shutting them still more to follow the writing, and handed it back to me, saying merely, "Pretty good."

"I'll leave it over at the E-A for him," I explained. "He thinks I'm afraid to go there alone."

"Yes. Pretty good," said McDonough, as if I were venturing nothing. Was all Wind River going to treat it as such a trifle? Or— could it be that McDonough alone among white men and red hereabouts knew nothing of the mystery and menace by which Still Hunt Spring was encircled?

Next morning my perplexity was cleared. I made an early start, tying some food and a kettle and my "slicker" to the saddle. McDonough watched me curiously.

"Leavin' your wagon and truck?" he inquired.

"Why, yes, of course. I'll be back for it. I'm going to the E-A now. Are you a poet?" I continued. "I've begun a thing." And I handed him some unfinished lines, which I had entitled "At Gift Horse Ranch." "You don't object to that?"

"Object to what?"

"Why, the title, 'At Gift Horse Ranch.' "

He took the paper down from his eyes, and I saw that his face had suddenly turned scarlet. He stood blinking for a moment, and then he said:—

"I'd kind of like to hear it."

"But that's all there is to hear—so far!" I exclaimed, feeling somehow puzzled.

He put the verses close to his eyes once more. Then he held them out to me, and stood blinking in his odd, characteristic way. "Won't y'u read 'em to me?" he at length managed to say. "I'll not fool *you*."

For yet one moment more I was dull, and did not understand.

"I can't read," he stated simply.

"Oh!" I murmured in mortification. And so I read the lines to him.

He stretched out his hand for the scribbled envelope on which I had pencilled the fragment. "May I keep that?"

"Wait till I have it finished."

"I'd kind of like to have the start to keep." He took it and shoved it awkwardly inside his coat. "I can't read or write," he said, more at his ease now the truth was out. "Nobody ever taught me nothin'."

But I was not at ease. "Well, that stuff of mine is not worth reading!" I said. Cards had a meaning for him—kings, queens, ten-spots—these had been the fellow's only books! He went on, "Never had any folks, y'u see—to know 'em, that is.—Well, so-long till you're back." He turned to his cabin, and I touched my horse.

The sorrel had gone but a few steps when I looked over my shoulder, and there stood the solitary figure, watching me from the cabin door. Suddenly it occurred to me that, as he had not been able to read my letter to Scipio, he knew nothing of my project. *This* was why he had manifested no surprise! "Do you think," I called back, laughing, "that your horse can take me to Still Hunt Spring?"

I am now sure that a flash of some totally different expression crossed his face, but at the time I was not sure; he was instantly smiling. "Take y'u anywhere," he called. "Take y'u to Mexico, take y'u to Hell!"

"Oh, not yet!" I responded, and cantered away. So he thought I would not dare to go alone to Still Hunt Spring! Well and good; they should all believe it by Friday evening.

My cantering ceased soon,—it had been for dramatic effect,—and as I had before me a long ride, it behooved me to walk the first miles. Yet I was soon up the easy ascent from North Fork, and though my descent to the main river from the dividing ridge was through precipitous red bluffs, and accomplished with caution, I reached the E-A ranch (where it used to be twenty-five years ago) in less than two hours. To leave my note there for Scipio took but a minute, and now on the level trail down Wind River I made good time, so that before ten o'clock I had crossed back over it above the Blue Holes, skirted by where the Circle fence is to-day, crossed North Fork here, gone up a gulch, and dropped down again upon Wind River below its abrupt bend, and reached the desolate Sand Gulch. I nooned at the spring which lies, no bigger than a hat, about seven miles up the Sand Gulch on its north side. This was the starting-point of the trail that old Washakie had drawn for me; here I crossed the threshold of the mysterious and the untrodden.

The sense of this heightened the elation which my ride through the bracing hours of dawn had brought me, and as I turned out of the Sand Gulch it was as if some last tie of restraint had stepped from my spirit, leaving it on wings free and rejoicing. This gleamy, unfooted country always looked monotonous from the bluffs of Wind River, but I found no tedium in it; its delicious loneliness was thrilled at each new stage of the trail by recognizing the successive signs and land-marks which Washakie had bidden me look for. The first was a great dull red stone, carved rudely by some ancient savage hand to represent a tortoise. Perhaps in another mood, the grim appearance of this monster might have seemed a symbol of menace, but when I came upon the stone just where my map indicated that it was to be expected, I hailed it with triumph. Nor did the caked and naked earth of the region through which I next traced my way dry up my ardor. Gullies sometimes hid all views from me, and again from mounds and rises I could see for fifty miles. Far off, but constantly in plain sight to my left, were Black Mountain and Spring Mountain; I must have been headed toward a point about midway between where the mail camp now is and the pass over to Embar. I crossed Crow Creek, next Dry Creek, and saw both Steamboat Butte and Tea Pot Butte at different points. As the hours of silence wore on, my elation settled to a contented serenity.

After the tortoise came several guiding
signs: a big gash in the soil, cut by a cloud-
burst; an old corral where I turned sharp to
the left; a pile of white buffalo bones five
miles onward; until at length I passed
through a belt of low hills, bare and baked and
colored, some pink, like tooth-powder, and
others magenta, and entered a more level
region covered with sparse grass and sage-
brush. Great white patches of alkali, acres in
extent, lay upon this plain. There was no
water—Washakie had told me there would be
none—and the gleamy waste stretched away
on all sides; endlessly in front, and right and
left to long lines of distant mountains, full of
light and silence. In the relentless blaze of
the day a curious shadow had begun to dim
my serenity. The gleamy waste seemed less
friendly and a strain of music, harsh and
ominous, set itself going, over and over, in my
mind. It sounded like what I was seeing:

a brooding landscape, grand and grave with
suggestion of ages unknown, of eras when the
sea was not where it is now, and animals
never seen by man wandered over the half-
made world. Earth did not seem one's own
here, but alien, but aloof, as if, through some
sudden translation, one had lit upon another
planet, perhaps a dying one. I rode forward
across the waste, and I tried to complete the
verses which I had begun at McDonough's:—

> Would I might prison in these words,
> And so keep with me all the year
> Some inch of this bright wilderness
> Of freedom that I move in here.

But nothing resulted from it, unless a surpris-
ingly swift flight of time. I was aware all at
once that day was gone, that the rose and saf-
fron heavens would soon be a field of stars. I
had matched one by one the signs on my map
with the realities around me, and now had
reached the map's last word; I was to stop
when I found myself on a line between a hol-
low dip in the mountains to the left and a
circular patch of forest high up on those to
the right. On this line I was to travel to the
right "a little way," said Washakie. This I
began to do, wondering if the twilight would
last, and for the first time anxious. After "a

little way" I found nothing new—the plain, the sage-brush, the dry ground—no more; and again a little further it was the same, while the twilight was sinking, and disquiet grew within me. Lost I could not well be, but I could fail; food would give out, and before this the sorrel and I must retrace our way to water at the Sand Gulch, seven hours behind us. The twilight deepened. Had I passed it? Should I ride in a circle? Rueful thoughts of a "dry camp" began to assert themselves, and my demoralized hand grew doubtful on the reins, when I gradually discovered that the sorrel *knew where he was.* There was no mistaking the increasing alertness that passed through him.

As this extraordinary fact became a certainty the chasm opened at my feet; the sorrel was trotting quickly along the brink of Still Hunt Spring! In broad day I should have seen it a moment sooner, and the suddenness with which, in the semi-obscurity, it had leaped into my view close beside me produced a startling effect. The success of my quest did not bring the unmixed pleasure that I had looked for; the dying day, the desolate shapes of the hills, the unbefriending hush of the plain, the odd alertness of the sorrel—all this

for a while flavored my triumph with something akin to apprehension, and it seemed as
if the ravine beneath me had been lurking in a
sort of ambush until I should be fully within
its power. The Indian legend was now easy to
account for; indeed, I have met often enough,
among our unlettered and rustic white pop-
ulation, with minds that would have believed,
after such a shock as I had just received,
that they had beheld the earth open supernat-
urally. The sorrel's trot had become a canter
as we continued to skirt the brink. Looking
down I discovered in shadowy form the line
of tall cottonwoods, spindled from their usual
shape to the gaunt figures described as being
on stilts; then the horse turned into the entrance. This steep and narrow trail was
barred at a suitable place by a barrier of
brush, which I replaced after passing it. A
haunting uneasiness caused me to regret that
I had not arrived in full daylight, but this
I presently overcame. Before we reached the
bottom I saw a number of horses grazing
down among the trees, and they set up a great
running about and kicking their heels at the
sight of a human visitor. There must have
been twenty or thirty.

Lassitude and satisfaction now divided my

sensations as I made my way to the spring,
whose cool, sweet water fulfilled all expecta-
tion. My good map served me to the last;
with it I lighted my cooking fire, addressing
it aloud as I did so, "Burn! your work is
done!" I needed no map to go back! I had
mastered the trail! In my recovered spirits
I quite forgot how much I owed to the sorrel.
While picking up dry sticks I stumbled upon
what turned out to be a number of branding
irons, which were quite consistent with the
presence of the horses and the barrier at the
entrance. Evidently the place sometimes
served as a natural pasture and corral for
stock gathered on the round-up and far
strayed from where they belonged. Perhaps
some one was camping here now. I shouted
several times; but my unanswered voice
merely made the silence more profound, and
for a while the influence of the magic legend
returned. With this my fancy played not
unpleasingly while the kettle—or rather the
coffee-pot—was boiling. The naturalness of
building a fire, of making camp, of preparing
a meal, helped common sense to drive out and
keep out those featureless fears which had
assailed me. What stories could be made
about this place by a skilful writer! The lost

traveller stumbles upon it, enters, suspects himself to be not alone, calls out, and immediately the haunted walls close and he is shut within the bowels of the earth. How release him? Therein would be the story. Or—the lost traveller, well-nigh dead of thirst, hastens to the spring amid the frolicsome gambols of the horses. No sooner has he drunk than he becomes a horse himself, and the others neigh loud greetings to a brother victim. Then a giant red man appears and brands him. How release all the horses from the spell?

As I lay by my little cooking fire in the warm night, after some bacon and several cups of good tea made in the coffee-pot, I was too contented to do aught in the way of exploration, and I continued to recline, hearing no sound but the grazing horses, and seeing nothing but the nearer trees, the dark sides of the valley, and the open piece of sky with its stars. My saddle-blanket and "slicker" served me for what bed I needed, the saddle with my coat supplied a pillow, and the cups of tea could not keep me from immediate and deep slumber.

I opened my eyes in sunlight, and the first object that they rested upon was a maroon-colored straw hat. With the mental confusion that frequently attends a traveller upon first waking in a new place, I lay considering the hat and wondering where I was, until at a sound I turned to see the hat's owner stooping to the spring. Instantly Lem Speed, cattleman and owner of a store and bank in Lander, a house in Salt Lake, a wife in Los Angeles, and a son at Yale, was covering me with a rifle.

"Stay still," was his remark.

Not a suspicion that it was anything but a joke entered my head. I lay there and I smiled. "I could not hurt you if I wished to."

"You will never hurt me any more."

Another voice then added: "He is not going to hurt any of us any more."

"Stay still!" sharply reiterated Lem Speed, for at the second voice I had half risen.

"For whom do you take me?" I asked.

"For one of the people we want."

I continued to be amused. "I'll be glad to know what you want me for. I'll be glad to know what damage I've done. I'll be happy to make it good. I came over here last night for—"

"Go on. What did you come for?"

"Nothing. Simply to see this place. I've wanted to see it for a year. I wanted to see if I could find it by myself." And I told them who I was and where I lived.

"That's a good one, ain't it?" said a third man to Lem Speed.

"And so," said he, "you, claiming you're an Eastern tenderfoot, found this place, first trip, all by yourself across fifty miles of country old-timers get lost in?"

"No. Washakie gave me a map."

"Let's see your map."

"I lighted my fire with it."

Somebody laughed. There were now five or six of them standing round me.

"If some of you gentlemen will condescend to tell me what you think my name is, and what you think I have done—"

"We don't know what your name is, and we don't care. As to what you've done, that's as well known to you as it is to us, and you've got gall to ask, when we've caught you right on the spot, branding-irons and all."

"Well, I'm beginning to understand. You think you've caught a cattle thief."

"Horse thief," corrected one.

"Both, probably," added another.

"I'll not ask you to believe me any more," I now said. "Don't I see the post-trader over there among those horses?"

"No."

"Very well, take me to him at Washakie. He has known me for years. I demand it."

"We'll not take you anywhere. We're going to leave you here."

And now the truth, the appalling, incredible truth, which my brain had totally failed to take in, burst like a blast over my whole being, penetrating the innermost recesses of my soul with a blinding glare. They intended to put me to death at once; their minds were as stone vaults closed against all explanation. Here in this hidden crack of the wilderness my body would be left hanging, and far away my family and friends would never know by what hideous outrage I had perished. Slowly they would become anxious at getting no news of me; there would be an inquiry, a mystery, then sorrow, and finally acceptance of my unknown fate. Broken visions of home, incongruous minglings of loved faces and commonplace objects, like my room with its table and chairs, rushed upon me. Had I not been seated, I must have fallen at the first shock of this stroke. They stood watching me.

"But," I began, feeling that my very appearance was telling against me, while my own voice sounded guilty to my ears, "but it's not true."

"What's the use in him talking any more to us?" said a man to Lem Speed.

Lem Speed addressed me. "You claim this:

you're an Eastern traveller. You come here—
out of curiosity. You risk getting lost in the
hardest country around here—out of curiosity. But you come all straight because an Indian's map guides you, only you've burnt it.
And you're a stranger, ignorant that this is
a *cache* for rustlers. That's what you claim.
It don't sound like much against these facts:
last year you and another man that's wanted
in several places and that we're after now—
you and him was known to be thick. You
offered to pay his doctor's bill. You come
back to the country where he's been operating
right along, and first thing you do you come
over to this *cache* when he's got stolen horses
right in it, and you ride a stolen horse that's
known to have been in his possession, and
that's got on it now the brand of the outfit
this gentleman here represents—all out of
curiosity.''

''We've just found six more of our stock
in here,'' said the gentleman indicated by
Speed.

I repeated my story in a raised voice—I
had not yet had time to regain composure.
I accounted for each of my movements from
the beginning until now, vehemently reassert-
ing my ignorance and innocence. But I saw

that they were not even attending to me any longer; they looked at me only now and then, they spoke low to each other, pointing to the other end of the valley, and turned, while I was still talking, to receive the report of another man, who came from among the stolen horses.

Then I fell silent. I sat by my saddle, locking my hands round my knees, and turning my eyes first upon the men, and then upon the whole place. A strange crystal desolation descended upon me, quiet and cold. The early sunlight showed every object in an extraordinary and delicate distinctness; the stones high up the sides of the valley, the separate leaves on the small high branches of the cottonwoods; the interstices on the bark on lower trunks some distance away; the fine sand and grass of the valley's level bottom, with little wild rose bushes here and there; all these things I noticed, and more, and then my eyes came back to my little dead fire, and the blackened coffee-pot in which I had made the tea. "Your friend McDonough," they had said to me at Washakie, and I had wondered what was behind their reticence when I inquired about him. They were always ready, I bitterly reflected, to feed lies to a tenderfoot, but a syllable of truth about McDonough's suspected dishonesty, which would have saved me from this, they were unwilling to speak. It was natural, of course; everything was natural. I saw also why McDonough had been so precise in asking which way I expected to travel. Over on Snake River, and in Idaho, the sorrel was in no danger of identification, and therefore I should be safe. But even with the whole chain of evidence: the doctor's bill, the corral, my unlucky tale of a map which I could not prove, and the branding-irons with which they believed I was going to alter the legitimate brands—what right had they to deny me the chance I asked?

The last two of them now came from the horses to make their report: "Five brands. Thirty-two head. N lazy Y, Bar Circle Zee, Goose Egg, Pitch Fork, Seventy-Six, and V R."

"Not one of you," I broke out, "knows a word against me, except some appearances which the post-trader will set right in one minute. I demand to be taken to him."

"Ain't we better be getting along, Lem?" said one.

"Most eight o'clock," said another, looking at his watch.

"Stand up," said Lem Speed.

Upon being thus ordered, like a felon, my utterance was suddenly choked, and it was with difficulty that I mastered the tears which welled hotly to my eyes.

"Any message you want to write—"

"No!" I shouted.

"Then let's be getting along," said the first man.

"Any message I wrote you would not deliver; it would put a rope round your neck, too. And, Mr. Lem Speed, with your store, and bank, and house, and wife, and son, I wish them all for your sake all the misfortune that life can bring."

A horse was led to me, and I got on without aid, a man on each side of me. We must have been some time—I think we walked—in reaching the other end of the valley, yet I cannot recall what was spoken around me, or whether or not anything was spoken; I can recall only the sides of the valley passing, and the warmer sense of the sun on my shoulders, and the vivid scent of the sage-brush. Before we halted at the fatal tree of execution, and while my rage was still sustaining me, a noise of rattling stones caused us all to look upward, and there, galloping down the steep trail,

wildly waving and shouting to us, was Scipio
Le Moyne. It reeled through me! I was
saved!

He plunged into the midst of us at break-
neck speed, drew up so short that his horse
slid, and burst out furiously—not to my cap-
tors, but to me. ''You need a nurse!'' he cried
hoarsely. ''Any travelling you do should be
in a baby coach.''

Breath failed him, he sat in his saddle,
bowed over and panting, hands shaking, face
dripping with sweat, shirt drenched, as was
his trembling horse. After a minute he looked
at Speed. ''So I'm in time, by God! I've rid-
den all night. I'd have been here an hour
sooner only I forgot about the turn at the
corral. Here. That's the way I knowed it.''

He handed over my letter, left for him at
the E-A ranch. This, with a few words from
him, cleared me. All that I had declared was
verified; they saw what they had been about
to do.

''Well, now, well!'' exclaimed one, grinning.

''To think of us getting fooled that way!''
another remarked, grinning.

''But it's all right now,'' said a third, grinning.

"That's so!" a fourth agreed. "No harm done. But we had a close shave, didn't we?" And he grinned, too.

Lem Speed approached me. "No hard feelings," he said jocularly, and he held out his hand.

I turned to Scipio. "Tell this man that anything he wishes to say to me he will say through you."

Speed flushed darkly. Had he kept his temper, he could easily have turned my speech to ridicule. But such a manner of meeting him was novel to a man used to having his own brutal way wherever he went, and he was disconcerted. He spoke loudly and with bluster :—

"You said some things about my wife and son that don't go now."

This delivered him into my hands. Again I addressed Scipio. "Say that I wish his family no further misfortune; they have enough in having him for husband and father."

I think he would have shot me, but the others were now laughing. "He's called the turn on you, Lem. Leave him be. He's been annoyed some this morning."

They now made ready to depart with their recovered property.

"You and your friend will come along with us?" one said to Scipio.

"Thank you," I answered. "I have seen all that I ever wish to see of any of you."

And then suddenly I folded over and slid like a sack of flour from my horse. It had lasted longer than my nerves were good for; darkness engulfed me on the ground.

They had disappeared when I waked; Scipio and I were the only human tenants of the valley. He sat watching me, and I nodded to him; then silently shook my head at his question if I wanted anything. I lay gazing at the rocks and trees, the tall trees with their leaves gently stirring. It was a beautiful, serene spot and I regarded it with the languid pleasure of a man recovering from a serious illness. We began to talk presently, and I learned that they had taken away their stolen horses, except the sorrel, which had been left at my complete disposal. But from that party I would accept no amends; I would ride the sorrel back to Wind River, and then I would send a check to the proper person, as if I had hired the horse. Scipio upbraided me with the spirit I was showing; they had meant no harm to *me*, he argued; they were doing their best now— but I turned upon him.

"Oh, their best! Do you think they'll not break out in a new place, condemn some other man who looks guilty to their almighty minds? I asked to see the post-trader. Don't forget that. There's got to be lynching where there's no law, but—"

To these unfinished words Scipio could find no answer, but he remained unconvinced, muttering that "tenderfeet shouldn't monkey with this country by themselves"; and in this sentiment I heartily concurred.

We spent the day and night at Still Hunt Spring. There was nothing to call us away, and I found my physical powers more inclined to rest than to a long ride. Scipio dried out his clothes beside the spring, and refreshed his lank body from the perspiration and dust which had covered it. He told me how it had been whispered that the cattlemen were on the eve of "demonstrating"; how McDonough's practices and associates had been gradually ascertained; how it was known that Still Hunt Spring had become a hiding-place for stolen stock. Therefore my bragging letter, written in a spirit so light, had given him what he described as "considerable of a jolt." He had not found it until evening, and had instantly galloped forth into the dark, not knowing what he might find at Still Hunt Spring.

"Then McDonough is a thief," I sighed.

"Oh, he's a thief all right," said Scipio easily.

But it made me very sad. I closed my eyes and could see McDonough as he stood by my horse, embarrassed, reaching out his hand for that envelope with my verses on it.

I slept more soundly and longer even than on the preceding night. Scipio, after his hard ride, slept like me; we did not wake until the sun was high and warm. After breakfast—it was the last morsel we had between us—I took a final drink at the gentle and lovely pool where I had undergone such terrible emotions, and we rode slowly and silently down the long line of trees toward the exit of the valley. Suddenly the sorrel jerked his head up, stopped stiff with a snort, and began to tremble. Ahead of us there, from the branch destined for me, hung a dead man, McDonough. This they had done while we overslept by the spring at the upper end of the valley. They had surprised him coming to his *cache*.

Scipio and I sat still for a while. A wind in the branches now set the body slightly swaying; it seemed worse when it moved; it turned half-way round, and I saw its eyes. "I think —couldn't we bury it?" I said.

Scipio shook his head. "It's left there for some of his partners to see."

"Well—I think we might close the eyes."

"That's no harm," said Scipio, "if you want."

"Yes; I do want."

So we dismounted. Yes; cards were all Mc-Donough knew how to read; no one had ever taught him anything; this was his first lesson.

"There," said Scipio, "that does look better." Then we rode away from Still Hunt Spring.

VI

ILE-HIGH in space circled a dark speck, a Mexican eagle, alone in the empty sky. He was looking down upon four hundred square miles of Arizona sand, called Repose Valley. He saw clots of cactus, thickets of mesquite, stunt oak bush, and white skeletons of cattle, but not a thing to eat. He also saw Aaron Tace, the shell-game man, in a Mexican hat. He also saw a man who, drifting lately to Tucson, had said his name was Belleville; but somebody in Tucson had pronounced this "Bellyful"; it was then vain to insist upon any other pronunciation.

Up in the sky sailed the eagle; along the desert road Aaron Tace was slowly riding; and on the ground lay Bellyful, near where the road forked to the mines. Aaron was going to Push Root. In that town a *fiesta* was being held; horses raced, liquors drunk, ladies courted, cards dealt, silver and gold lost by many and won by few, all to music. Bellyful was bound presently for Push Root, too. Now

176

he lay off the road under some mesquite,
thinking, while Aaron approached. Made of
thorns, slender rods, and gauze foliage, Bellyful's bushes cast little more shade than mos-
quito nets, but they cast all the shade there
was. He was resting his starved, weak horse,
whose legs must somehow walk the five more
miles to Push Root. He, himself, with scant
breakfast inside, had led the horse to the thin
shade. The poor beast stood over him; now
and then Bellyful reached up and stroked its
nose. At sunrise the softened mountains had
glowed like jewels, or ripe nectarines, or
wine; cooling shadows had flowed from them
upon the valley. Later morning had changed
these peaks to gray, hot teeth, and the sand
to a gray, hot floor. The horse rested, Aaron
Tace was half a mile nearer, the eagle sailed,
and Bellyful lay thinking of his luck.

He had known none in fifteen months. Misfortune bulged from the seams of his shirt and
trousers and boots. Of his gold watch, his two
pins, his ring, his sundry small possessions,
only his gun remained: he could not pawn the
seat of life. He had been earning and spending easily, when the first illness that he had
ever known put him to bed, and almost in his
grave. Coming back to strength, he found

hard times. No one, no railroad, ranch, restaurant, saloon, stage company—nothing—
had employment for him. He had sought it
from San Marcial, over in New Mexico, west-
ward to Yuma, hundreds of miles. He had
parted early with his real name. On a freight
train at Bowie the conductor found him steal-
ing a ride, and kicked him off, calling him a
hobo. The epithet hurt worse than the kick.
In fact, hiding on the brake-beam under another car—for in spite of the conductor he
carried out his plan of riding free to Willcox
—he shed tears, the bitter tears of pride de-
parting; he *was* a hobo. By the time he
reached Willcox, Belleville was his name. No
tramp should be called what his mother had
named him.

Such his life had been; dust, thirst, hunger,
repulse—and onward to more. Existence
shook her head at him with a changeless
"No." Latterly, in Tucson, a pretty woman
had shown him kindness which she should not,
since he was not her husband and she had one.
She fell in love with the April bloom of his
years and with his hard luck—and this was
the single instance of human interest in him
which had touched his life in fifteen months.
It lay light upon his roving conscience, was

nothing but joy and pride to him; but his
code forbade continued acceptance of her
money that there seemed no chance to repay.
Quitting Tucson, he took from her, as a final
loan, enough to buy a wretched horse, with a
trifle over. If none in Push Root would em-
ploy him, the mines were left; if these should
fail, then he would have knocked at the door
of every trade in Arizona, except robbery,
which was undoubtedly the territory's chief
industry.

Bellyful slid down a hand to his pocket's
bottom. One by one he fingered seven coins
therein, his whole fortune, in fractional cur-
rency—it summed up to a dollar and four
bits. He drew out the coins and attentively
read their dates. These he already knew. He
was not thinking of the coins, but of the Universe, and how successfully it resisted explanation. A voice stopped him; Aaron Tace
was nearly opposite his clump of mesquite.
The shell-game man was talking to himself.

"Remember, gentlemen, the hand is quicker
than the eye." This he said over and over,
while his hands were ceaselessly moving. Bellyful rose with astonishment, and stared.
Aaron Tace could easily have seen him, but

was too busy. He was making quick turns and passes, and talking the while.

"Remember, gentlemen, the hand is quicker than the eye." Nothing but that, while his hands paused, shuffled, and paused again.

"Remember, gentlemen—" It was like a player polishing his lines. Aaron rehearsed all the tones that express complete candor and friendly warning, with a touch of "dare you to try it!" thrown in. The reins hung on the horse's neck. Fitted to the saddle-horn (a very neat piece of work) was a smooth, wooden tray, and upon this three walnut shells in a line. These Aaron Tace would shift from right to left and back, or half back, exchanging their positions, sliding them among each other, lifting them up and setting them down—a pretty thing to see. Only one slip he made, due to a stumble of his horse. The little pebble, or pea, which the shifted shells concealed by turns to allure the bets of onlookers, rolled to the ground. Aaron sprang off limberly, found it, and was on again, busily rehearsing while his horse walked onward. He had now passed by, and a rock hid him from view; but for a long time still Bellyful could hear the rising and falling cadence of his "Remember, gentle-

men, the hand is quicker than the eye,'' even
after the syllables ceased to be distinguish-
able. Thus Aaron proceeded toward the Push
Root *fiesta,* happy and busy, until his distant
cadences died away.

''Well, I'll be damned,'' said Bellyful.

For perhaps an hour he lay, looking upward through the filmy mesquite, himself a
piece of the vast silence. But this new light
on the shell game helped little to render the
Universe more susceptible of explanation.
By and by he took his slow way along the
road, and nothing living was left at the Forks.
Far in the huge, blue, hot sky the eagle sailed,
hunting his prey.

.   .   .   .

Bellyful found the town of Push Root full
of good nature. Indeed, there was more good
nature than town; it spilled over the edges in
strains of music, strains of language, and
gentlemen overcome in the brush. But it was
beyond the livery stable's good nature to
trust any such looking owner of any such looking horse; Bellyful paid in advance. He inquired for employment at the stage office,
the hardware store, the other store, the
Palace Hotel, the other hotel, the Can-Can

Restaurant, the Fashion Saloon, the four
other saloons, and the three private houses.
These were locked because their owners were
out, practising good nature. That finished it;
there was no employment here. The horse
could never make the mines without two
meals and a night's rest—paid for already.
No duty now hindered Bellyful from being
good-natured himself. He still had three
coins of slight importance to do it with, and
his absent-minded fingers rubbed them over
in his pocket.

Push Root teemed with strangers from
ranch and mine, wandering joyously between
drinks in search of new games. Through the
many sounds Aaron's voice held its own, and,
reaching Bellyful, waked his brooding mind,
which had long forgotten Aaron. Some
games he knew about, but this one had hitherto not been closely studied by him. Was
the eye always slower than the hand? Practice makes perfect, but—? With this dawn
of scientific doubt Bellyful stood looking at
the cluster of patrons which screened Aaron
where he shuffled his three walnut shells and
chanted his "Remember, gentlemen." A dis-
ordered-looking patron now emerged from the
group, perceived Bellyful, lurched toward

him, leaned against him confidingly, and remarked with tears:—

"Say, are you married? I am. Some people are fools all the time. I am. All people
are fools some of the time. I am. And when
I get home I'll get hell." He untied an old
horse and rode desolately out of town.

Through the air, like a call, came Aaron's
jaunty voice. Bellyful joined the patrons at
once. Aaron shot over him a travelled, measuring eye, of which the not untravelled Bellyful took prompt note. He stood in the front
row, staring with as simple an expression as
he could command, slowly fumbling the poor
little coins in his pocket. Soon the man next
him won three dollars on a dime. Bellyful
came near whistling, but repressed it in order
to maintain his simple expression. Thirty to
one! This game paid thirty to one! And the
dawn of scientific doubt grew lighter.

"Try yourn." This suggestion somebody
made to a youth of prosperous appearance,
with an English neatness, and a cap and
waistcoat of the horse-stable variety.

"Thanks, no, ye know. Seen it with thim-
bles at home, ye know."

None present was aware that this accent
had been heard in no part of the British Isles

at any time. Yet, after a look at him, Bellyful's scientific doubt dawned a trifle clearer.

"Win three dollars?" cried an astonished
freighter.

"Remember, gentlemen, the hand is quicker
than the eye," said Aaron, instantly.

He shuffled his shells. The freighter's hairy
fist made a "jeans dive." This well-known
reach for money in the "pants" is composed
of two gestures: the hand shoots down into
the pocket, while the head tilts skyward. It
is common where hay grows, and often fore-
tells that the owner and his money will soon
be parted. Bellyful now forgot all about his
empty stomach. The freighter touched a shell,
put down five cents, and won a dollar and a
half.

"Megod!" exclaimed British Isles. He
risked a quarter, and lost.

"Aw, now!" he lamented. "Good-by, all."

They rallied him, chaffed him, told him to
come back and be a man; so, not to shame old
England in a foreign country (as he explained), he doubled his quarter, and lost
again.

"Remember, gentlemen," chanted Aaron,
"the hand is quicker than the eye."

He shuffled the shells straight at the

freighter, as if he were making love to him.
The freighter's eyes bulged; he dredged from
his pocket a sort of bun of bills, greasy old
rags pressed to a lump, gazed at them,
touched them, smoothed them, and at last,
amid general laughter, shoved them linger-
ingly back into his jeans. But his eyes seemed
unrestful, and he mopped his brow.

"She's there!" bet British Isles, touching
a shell.

"Take you," said Aaron.

British Isles put a dollar down. The pea
was under the shell. Everybody saw the
thirty dollars paid to British Isles. Aaron
shuffled his shells anew.

"She's there!" thundered the freighter.
His hand shot down, his head tilted up, and
out came the bun again. A neighbor moved
a gentle elbow against the freighter's ribs,
and silently indicated another shell. In his
excitement Bellyful now nearly forgot to keep
looking innocent. The dawn of scientific doubt
showed signs of sunrise; if this freighter
should *lose,* all would be known to Bellyful
but one last detail. If the freighter should
win—why, then, a splendid theory went up
in smoke.

The neighbor pushed a little harder with

his elbow. This time the freighter felt it. He backed away from the neighbor with glaring indignation.

"Ho, no, young man!" he exclaimed loudly. "Keep your tips for greenhorns that ain't on to this game." He flayed twenty dollars off his bun. "She's under there," he declared tapping his own shell again.

"Take you," said Aaron. He lifted the shell. No pea was there!

"Aw!" commented British Isles sympathetically. "Come again, sir. You'll be apt to swat him next time."

But the unhappy freighter stood still in an ox-like bewilderment, turning large, rueful eyes now upon the shuffling shells and now upon the neighbor, whose lip curled with a cold, wise smile.

Scientific doubt was rosy everywhere; full knowledge might break at any minute. Bellyful knew now that the freighter was too innocent to be true, that he was in it with Aaron, in it with British Isles, that the three of them had a united eye upon some fat quarry, and were playing a game to bag him. Who was it? Bellyful looked at every man.

"Are you on yet?" whispered the neighbor, edging up. While the bets and shuffling went

on, he whispered wisdom behind his hand to
Bellyful. Aaron won steadily in a small way
till a lull in business came; this he cured by
losing sixty well-timed dollars to British
Isles. Small business picked up at once.
Some people are fools all the time, all
people are fools some of the time—but when
was the fat quarry coming? Every little while
the neighbor dropped more expert wisdom
into Bellyful's ear. "A bad thing," he whispered, "ever to take your eye off the shells.
While that hayseed freighter was looking at
the sky, just now, the shells had been changed
round. Hard to prove it, too, even if you
thought you saw it. Best way of all was, keep
your hand on the shell you bet on. Don't let
him move it and talk, for even if the pea was
under it he could get it away. He'd never let
you win if he didn't want you to. Keep your
hand on your shell."

"H'm," answered Bellyful.

"Here's the real trick," continued the expert neighbor. "He shuffles till he sees by
your eye you've spotted a shell. Maybe he
leads you on to spot a shell by playing awkward. And he claps down the shell."

"H'm," responded Bellyful again.

"No. I hadn't finished," explained the

expert. "Of course the pea is not under that shell. Where is it? Nestling in his little right finger. Some of 'em is both-handed and can work two peas. So, when you bet, no pea is under any shell. You're bound to lose, see? And see how he holds his shells with them two end fingers crooked in and how he stoops over 'em close to the edge of the table now and then."

"H'm," unchangeably remarked Bellyful.

"Yes, but you ain't watching," complained the expert. "When he scrapes a shell close to the edge, that's when the pea's liable to tumble into his little finger. I'm going after him in a minute."

A flash came into Bellyful's eye. He turned his head for one look at the expert. It satisfied him.

"I guess you're catching on now," said the expert. "There! The pea's in his finger. Watch me."

Bellyful watched.

The expert had gold pieces, plenty of them, all sizes. He put down five dollars. "I'll pick up," he said, "the two shells the pea's not under."

"Take you," said Aaron.

The expert quickly picked up two shells. But the pea was under one of them.

"You win," said Aaron instantly, and instantly caught up all three shells and shuffled them. One hundred and fifty dollars to the expert, though he had really lost! "See what that means?" he whispered to Bellyful. "He paid me not to expose him."

"H'm," replied Bellyful.

"Watch me again," urged the expert.

Indeed, Bellyful did. Scientific doubt was over; the full sun had risen.

Once more the shuffled shells came to rest, enticing bets, when violent voices arose off to the left. Aaron quite—oh, quite!—forgot, and looked away to see what the noise was. The freighter quickly lifted a shell. The pea was there. He clapped the shell down.

"Put your hand on that, young man," he commanded. "She's there," he shouted to Aaron, whose eye now had come back. The disturbance had been some brief trouble between British Isles and a man near him; it was quieted. The freighter bet the rest of his money—that large bun. The expert, with his hand on the shell, bet all his gold—it made several stacks.

"Take you," said Aaron.

The pea wasn't beneath the shell!

"Too bad, gentlemen," said Aaron, gathering promptly all the money and the shells, and shoving everything into his pockets. "Well, I told you the hand was quicker than the eye. Good-by! Better luck next time!" He nodded kindly, and was gone.

The game was done, the patrons dispersed. British Isles and the freighter no longer to be seen, everybody melted away among the wagons, the horses, the people, the sounds, the shows, the music of the general *fiesta*. On the deserted spot stood the expert and Bellyful, looking at each other.

"What are you trembling about?" demanded the expert, sharply.

"I don't know," said Bellyful. He didn't know.

"Five hundred and thirty-five dollars," muttered the expert, hoarsely. "That freighter got the pea out when he scraped that shell down."

"They were all three laying for you from the start," said Bellyful. He couldn't stop trembling. Perhaps it was want of food.

"Five hundred and thirty-five dollars," wailed the expert.

After that, he, too, melted away.

.   .   .   .

Five miles out of Push Root, where the road forks to the mines, nothing had changed, except the name of the day. Repose Valley had not aged in twenty-four hours; it may be doubted if Repose Valley could have looked older in twenty-four million hours. Its sand was hot and gray, its mountains were hot and gray, its sunlight glared like a curse. No breeze, no water, no shade; gauze mesquite, stiff cactus, white cattle bones—four hundred square miles of this, quite as usual. It might just as well have been yesterday, but for its name. All the days of the week here might have sat for each other's photographs. Only the Creator could have told them apart. Up in the blue air sailed the eagle. Evidently he must find meals in Repose Valley, else he wouldn't be here, sailing and watching. He saw the same horse and the same Bellyful resting beneath the same mesquite. He saw also, away off, the same Aaron riding slowly along the road toward the Forks—only, this morning, Aaron was coming from Push Root instead of going to it. This proved it wasn't yesterday. Aaron had out his practice-table, and his hands were industrious.

Again Bellyful lay thinking. His horse was better for the hay and corn and eighteen hours of rest; but the mines were further than Push Root, and he must get there, there was nowhere else left to get—except *out!* As he lay under the mesquite, Bellyful made one gesture—he shook his fist at the sky. They might put him out, but he wouldn't get out.

It might be said that the only difference between the Bellyful of yesterday and him of to-day was the difference of one dollar and four bits. He had nothing now in his pocket; those last coins had paid for what food they could buy him. But there was another difference. It had been wrought during the night hours, wrought while he lay in the stable, unable to sleep, possibly wrought also, even in the sleep he at length fell into just before daylight; for, while he slept, his heart went on beating, of course, and what was his soul doing?

After his single gesture he lay under the mesquite motionless, gazing up through the filmy branches, quiet as a stone, deep sunk in the heart of Repose Valley silence. Stretched so, still beneath the same mesquite, he looked as if he had been there since yesterday, as if in all the to-morrows he might be there, keeping the cattle bones company. But the whole boy—every inch of flesh and spirit—was alive, very much alive, not at all in a moderate, everyday fashion; in fact Bellyful was a powder magazine, needing nothing but a match. Existence had shaken her head at him once too often.

He didn't suspect his own state until the match was applied. Aaron's approaching voice reached him. Even the eagle, a mile up in the air, stopped hunting to witness the sudden proceedings. Bellyful leaped to his feet, looked at the rock which blocked him and his horse from Aaron's view, moved the passive beast a few paces back, looked at the rock again, was satisfied, ran like wild game behind the rock, and waited. His pistol was always in excellent order, a clean-polished, incongruous gleam to flash forth from such a rusty scarecrow.

The talking Aaron came along, happy and busy. His head bent over his shuffled shells; the rise and fall of his cadences grew clearer, the sounds began to take to themselves syllables; first "hand" and "eye" came out distinct, then the links between filled in, and the whole sentence rang perfect through the unstirred air.

"Remember, gentlemen, the hand is quicker than the eye."

Such rehearsals as this must have helped many a monotonous journey to pass pleasantly for Aaron—not to speak of placing him in the foremost ranks of Art.

"Remember, gentlemen, the hand is quicker than the eye."

"Not this morning."

The shells smashed in Aaron's horrified grasp. The little pea rolled to the ground.

"Going to the mines?" pursued Bellyful. All his words were sweet and dreadful.

Then Aaron saw behind the pistol who it was.

"That kid a road-agent!" he thought. "Why didn't I spot him yesterday?" And he blamed his own blindness, miserably and quite unjustly, because how could he know that Bellyful had only become a road-agent in the last ten minutes?

"Strip," said Bellyful.

Aaron was slow about it.

A flash, a smoke, and a hole through Aaron's Mexican hat cleared every doubt.

"You're mature, I see," remarked Aaron, and offered his unbuckled pistol.

"The other one now," commanded Bellyful. This was a guess, but a correct one. "Leave 'em both drop down."

Both dropped down.

"Go on strippin'."

The money followed, a good deal of it, and Aaron made a gesture of emptiness.

"That all?"

"Yes, indeed, young man."

"Then I want the rest of it."

"You've got the rest. You've got the whole. The game ain't what it used to be, and I have partners; they—"

"I'll partner you. Get down. Get down quick."

Evidently a compromise was the very most a poor shell-game man in this hapless crisis could hope for. Aaron got down and addressed the road-agent.

"See here, bo," he began, "you and me oughtn't to be hostile. In our trade we can't afford it. You and me's brothers."

"Don't you call me brother. I don't lie. I say 'hand it over' and folks ain't deceived. I'm an outlaw and, maybe, my life is forfeit. But you pretend you're an honest man and that your dirty game is square. Throw it all down, or I'll tear it out of you."

Aaron threw it all down. Then he was allowed to go his way, seeking more fools to cheat.

Up in the air the eagle sailed. He was still looking down upon clumps of cactus, thickets

of mesquite, and skeletons of cattle. He also
saw a horseman going slowly one way, and a
horseman going slowly the other. In time
many miles lay between them, and the forks
of the road were as silent and empty of motion as the rest of Repose Valley.

.   .   .   .

To me, listening, Scipio Le Moyne told the
foregoing anecdote while he lay in hospital,
badly crumpled up by a bad horse. Upon the
day following I brought him my written version.

"Yes," he said musingly, when I had finished reading it to him, "that—happened—
eight—years—ago. You've told it about correct—as to facts."

"What's wrong, then?"

"Oh—I ain't competent to pass on your
language. The facts are correct. What are
you lookin' at me about?"

"Well—the ending."

"Ending?"

"Well—I don't like the way Bellyful just
went off and prospered and—"

"But he did."

"And never felt sorry or—"

"But he didn't."

"Well—"

"D'you claim he'd oughtn't? Think of him! Will y'u please to think of him after that shell game? He begging honest work and denied all over, everywhere, till his hat and his clothes and his boots were in holes, and his body was pretty near in holes—think of him, just a kind of hollo' vessel of hunger lying in that stable while the shell-game cheat goes off with his pockets full of gold." Scipio spoke with heat.

"Yes, I know. But, if Bellyful afterward could only feel sorry and try—"

"Are you figuring to fix that up?"—he was still hotter—"because I forbid you to monkey with the truth. Because I *never* was sorry."

"*What?*"

"I was Bellyful," said Scipio, becoming quiet. "Yes, that was eight years ago." He mused still more, his eyes grew wistful. "I was nineteen then. God, what good times I have had!"

VII

WHEN Scipio had brought to an end the edifying anecdote, he lay in his hospital bed, silent and a little tired after so sustained a recital.

"Why not write," I inquired, "a book, and call it Tales From My Past?"

He looked at me suspiciously, but suspicion melted into what immediately sparkled in the tones of his reply. "In spite of my ancestors, I don't know French."

For an instant I was stupid—I have many such instants.

"You've often told me," he had to explain, "that in France y'u can print anything."

"Oh, well!" I laughed, "quite a number of yours are harmless enough—even for our magazines. This one for instance."

But his thoughts had gone on; he was gazing through the open window with a craving eye. All out-of-doors was his true home, his hearth and bed, his natural workshop and playground; indoors had been merely his occasional resort—a place where a man went for

198

a brief visit when he felt like spending his money. "I'm goin' to get well," he said, still watching the far-off, golden hills. "I *am* getting well. And wunst I'm on my legs I'll start makin' a lot more Past."

"Do!" I exclaimed. "Do. It isn't everybody who can, even when they try."

He grunted. "Huh! I ain't never tried much. Didn't have to. Things just kind o' seem to happen when I'm around."

"Did you lie just now?" I asked.

"Lie? When?"

"Didn't you fix up the ending?"

"Fix up nothin'! That's what them two old junipers actually did."

"You'll remember," I persisted, "you forbade me the other day to 'monkey with the facts,' when I told you I didn't like the ending of Bellyful's adventure in Repose Valley."

"Sure! Us Western men don't care about fixed-up things when we know how things are—when we've been the things ourselves. And will you tell me"—Scipio grew earnest —"what's the point of a book lyin' about life the way more'n half of 'em do? The way I wouldn't let y'u do about Bellyful?"

"Oh, our sincere and pious public is determined that virtue shall triumph in print, anyhow—and that nothing naked is **true** until draped.''

''Not me. I don't want any of them bib-and-tucker-and-safety-pin stories they hand you out. What made y'u think I'd lied?''

''Well, it seemed too good, too virtuous, too right.''

He grinned, and I perceived this to be at my expense—he had caught *me* taking divergent postures toward life and toward print.

''I surrender!'' I laughed. ''I'm a liar, too!''

His grin now faded. ''Now and then, y'u know, people do act decent. I've met several besides them two old men. Even along the Rio Grande. Why, I've acted decent myself at times.'' He seemed to review his recent anecdote. ''The point was,'' he said next, ''*they* always thought they were madder than they *were*. Now *I'm* just the other way. I'm that good-natured that I'm frequently madder than I feel—and it's the other man finds that out!''

''Get out of here!'' said the post doctor, entering. ''Look at your victim's eyes!''

So I went out, ashamed of myself at having led poor Scipio to talk so much. I needn't change a syllable of as many as I recollect in

his anecdote. His impression of the Thowmet Valley as it had been in those earlier
days—before apples, before the Great Northern, before anything—shall not be "fixed up"
by me.

I'd been seein' a lot of country, clear up
from Mazatlan to the Big Bend—driftin'
through Old Mexico and California and Awregon, and over for a little while to Boisé, and
up through the Palouse where the dust puffed
up from the ploughs and trailed like a freight-
train's smoke does on the Southern Pacific
for a half-hour after she's went by; and I'd
crossed the God-awful Big Bend—but I'll
skip that—and I'd crossed the stinkin', vicious Columbia on a chain ferry—but I'll skip
that—and I was kind o' tired. Didn't want no
mines either. There was mines up there and
folks crowdin' to 'em, thick from everywheres. But I was tired. Figured I'd put in
the balance of the fall—and the winter, too,
maybe—in some pleasant place, if they could
direct me to such a thing. So they told me
there was women—wives, I mean—and children and homes and neighbors over on the
Thowmet. So I headed for there. Went in
with a Siwash over the Chillowisp trail. Him

and me couldn't talk much, but we could nod
and point and grunt when his English and
my Chinook gave out. He carried the mail in
wunst a week, except when the snow wouldn't
let him. That proved to be often. Oh, but I
liked the Thowmet Valley's looks that first
sight! And it stayed pleasant to me. Why did
I leave it? Don't know. Just got curious to
see some more country.

There wasn't any homes to see as the Injun
and me rode down the hill. But trees that
could shade you, and grass a horse could eat,
and water not runnin' like it wanted to kill
you, but friendly water. And the mountains
all around was pleasant, too—timber on 'em.
Snow not on 'em yet, except a dozen or so
high-up, far-back patches, lyin' around white
like wash-day. So we rode along up the valley
and camped, and next day struck a cabin, and
corral and haystacks. Sure enough! Married
man with wife and kids. Kids had regular
Texas-colored hair. But the most homes was
farther up the river, they said, near the Forks
and store; and so I went along with the Siwash, who was bound for the store with his
mail-sack. The store was the post-office, of
course—Beekman was its name. We passed
by a tent 'side of the road, and voices was

screechin' inside the tent, and the Siwash he started to laugh. So I asked him what he knowed about it. Let me see. What did he say? I don't have use any more for the Chinook I learned up there. Oh, yes! He said:—

"Klaska tenas man, klaska hyas pilton."

So I didn't know what that meant, and there wasn't much good mentioning this to him; but I didn't have to, for they came a-rushin' out of the tent, no hats on.

"How does a coyote walk?" screeched out the littlest one, aimin' his finger at me.

Well, I felt huffy—never'd saw him before or his partner neither—didn't catch the joke —but he wasn't jokin'. The big one arrives and he yells:—

"Don't he walk separate?"

"He walks together, don't he?" yells the little one.

Little one had scrambled hair, white, and it hadn't been cut lately. Big partner had left his hair behind him somewheres along life's journey. They was glarin' up at me for an answer.

So I said: "Tell me what you mean."

So they did. They was trappers. One claimed you could always tell a coyote's tracks by the way he put his right foot and his left foot down in different places, so you could tell he was a four-footed animal; and the other he said that was the way the bob-cat and the lynx and the mountain-lion walked. And then the first one he yelled out that they stuck one foot right in the other foot's track, so it looked like a two-footed animal had been walkin' there.

"That's all easy," I said; for I've trapped some myself.

So I set 'em straight as to the facts. Thing was, they quieted down right off and took my say-so. But that was their way, I found—get up a regular state-of-things that would mean trouble, you'd suppose, and drop it as if no-body'd said a word.

"Come and finish dinner," says the little one to the big one.

"Dinner!" says the big one. "Quit your dining. You've eet enough to wake the dead."

So they starts back to their tent like twins. I expect they were sixty, or seventy, or eighty —I don't know how long they'd lasted in this world—and one had boots, and the other had his feet tied in gunnysack, and both looked like two-bits' worth of God-help-us.

But they didn't get to their tent that time. Down the road comes a nice-lookin' girl on a

calico horse with one blue eye—the horse had
—and the little one he sees her and he whirls
around and aims his finger at her, same as he
done to me.

"No, you don't!" says he, loud up in the
air. "I've told you I won't."

"I had no intention of speaking about it
again," says she, rather quiet, but smilin'.
"But when you find that there's no coal really
there—"

Well, what d'y'u think? It set 'em wild.
Both of 'em went plumb wild. I couldn't hear
for a while what the trouble was, because they
scrambled their words just like the little one's
hair, talkin' to the girl and me and the Siwash
and each other. But the Siwash he gave another laugh and rode away—he had his mail.
I stayed. I hadn't got used to 'em yet.
Thought maybe she'd better have a man
around. But they was absolutely harmless.
And then I began to understand.

The girl she sat there indulgin' 'em. Told
'em she wasn't goin' to worry 'em about it
any more. They told her there was coal there
and they was goin' to supply the whole valley,
and it was better than a gold-mine. She might
just as well have worried 'em instead of sittin' so peaceful on the calico horse, because

they would never have noticed any worryin'
she could do—they was that busy with the
worry they were keepin' up all by themselves.
She was a school-teacher and up to now she'd
kept school in a tent. But the valley was going to build a school-house and the best loca-
tion for it happened to be on some land they'd
filed on. Any other place would be too far
for somebody's kids, or for everybody's, or
else hadn't water convenient. But it seemed
they wouldn't hear of it. I suppose whoever
put it to 'em first had put it wrong, and now
all y'u had to do was say "school-house" in
their hearing, and have a circus prompt.

"Mr. Edmund," says she to me, "says that
if their idea of other minerals is like their
idea of coal, it's no wonder they have found
trapping more profitable. But no one can per-
suade them, and it's truly a pity about the
school-house." Mr. Edmund kept the store at
Beekman.

"If it's not coal," says I, "what is it?"

"Oh, slate, or graphite, or something—and
just a tiny ledge, and too far from transpor-
tation."

"Well, then, it don't burn."

"You can't reason with them," says she.
And she smiles down at them two quarrelin',

fussin' old men. It would have brought me
to reason, her smile would, but she never gave
it to me.

Yes, she indulged 'em. The valley indulged
'em right along. They was so old and so
harmless. Kultus Jake and Frisco Baldy was
their names—all the names I ever heard for
'em—and they'd been most everywheres before other people had. Been acrost the Isth-
mus and round the Horn, they claimed—not
together, y'u know, but they had met when
they was young. Their trails had crossed
somewheres in Sonora. Then they'd met
again on the Santa Fé trail, when they was
still young. And so now and then they'd kep'
a-meetin' and a-growin' less young. Been
through the gold excitement of '49. Drifted
up to Portland. Got separated at Klamath
about the time of the Modoc War. Didn't see
each other again till both come face to face
over in the Okanogan country—and then they
was old. They remembered former days, and
it tied 'em together. They was goin' to Africa
next time they felt like they needed a change
of air. Kultus Jake's hair was all the moss
he'd ever gathered, and Frisco Baldy he
seemed to have gathered nothin' whatever.
But they packed around a big harvest of

years—no one ever knowed the sum of it.
Wunst in a while they would speak of something they had done together long ago. Then
y'u knew the silent tie between 'em. I don't
wish to live that long and have to look backward when I want to see anything of promise.
It's awful when everybody has to indulge y'u
—time to quit then. But y'u needn't to pity
Kultus Jake and Frisco Baldy, for they was
just as set and cheerful about goin' to Africa
as young rich folks talkin' over what waterin'
place they'll visit next summer. Liveliest old
junipers that ever I see!

Kultus, y'u know, is Chinook, and it's used
for most anything that don't amount to
nothin'. And while we're on Chinook, here's
something funny. *Potlatch* means a gift. Now
you'd suppose *kultus potlatch* would be a poor
gift—counterfeit dollar or a dozen rotten
eggs, for instance. Well, you're wrong. You
give a man a bridle, or a hindquarter of veni-
son, or anything y'u choose, and say nothin'
when y'u give it—that's just a plain common
potlatch, and it means he's expected by all the
rules to give you something pretty soon,
something as good as your bridle or your
deer. But you say *"Kultus potlatch"* to him,
and then he'll be genuinely grateful, for that

means you're just makin' him a real present out of the warmness of your heart, and don't expect him to come back at y'u with a huckleberry for your persimmon. Why, when a Siwash—the custom came from them—gave me somethin' in silence, it used to worry me 'most to death.

What the mail-carrier said to me the first day, when the two old men was screechin' inside their tent, was that they were children and fools. But he was an Injun and did not have indulgent feelings. I saw more of 'em and didn't mind 'em. I fell into a job at the Forks. Mr. Edmund wanted somebody else in the store, and I could write a plain hand and add figures fairly correct. He was kind of mad about the school-house, havin' the interests of the valley at heart, and he used to watch the days gettin' shorter. Mr. Edmund had everything at heart—too much at heart—other folks' troubles as well as his own. He would lecture me about them in his deep-down voice. School wouldn't do in a tent after snow came, and he saw that this would come down to havin' school in his own cabin if the children was to get any teachin' at all. He was the only one that didn't leave 'em alone about their coal-mine. Offered to buy it off 'em wunst, and they screeched for ten minutes. Threatened to write to Washington and have him removed for takin' advantage of his office.

"Why, you don't know where Washington is," says he, with his voice down in the cellar.

"Washington, D. C.?" screeches Kultus Jake. "I don't know? I been there!"

"Washington, D. C.," repeats Edmund slow, like Fate a-comin'. "You don't know where it is." That was Edmund all over. His way o' jokin'.

"It's in Maryland," says Frisco Baldy.

"Virginia, y'u singed porcupine!" yells Kultus Jake. "Don't I tell y'u I been there?"

And I seen they both meant it. And I seen this really grieved Edmund instead of pleasin' him. He took it to heart. Well, sir, I just went acrost the store and lay down on the flour-sacks. Kicked up my heels. Guess I made more noise than the old men did. After a minute I lifted up to see what Edmund was doin', and he'd pushed his spectacles up high on his forehead and was lookin' at the two scrappin' about Washington, D.C., out of his awful solemn eyes; so I laid down again flat. If Edmund had talked I couldn't have heard him, but as a matter of fact he just let 'em go it alone; and they, like they pretty much always done, got switched off on to somethin' else—this time it was the traps. There was some number fours hanging there, and they both happened to agree it was number fours they would take when they started into the mountains to trap for the winter. So traps made 'em forget about Washington, D.C., and *it* had made 'em forget about exposin' Edmund, which had made 'em forget the coalmine and the school-house, and so they departed entirely peaceful out of the store and over the Thowmet to their tent, which they had moved up to the Forks. Then I looks up from the sacks again. There stands Edmund behind his desk, same as ever, spectacles away up on his forehead, only now his solemn eyes was fixed on me. And I looks at him, not knowin' what on earth he's goin' to say or whether he's mad or ain't mad—for y'u couldn't often tell from his face. For a young man—and he was young—he was a lot growed up. I expect he knew sorrow early. Both of us was quite silent.

"I didn't know they didn't know," says Edmund, like he was breaking the news of a death to y'u.

And I lays right down again on the sacks.

"Good Lord!" says Edmund, "what ignorance. The capital of their country!"

But I could only fight for my breath, and cry and cry.

Next time I could see anything, there was Edmund sittin' on the counter clost alongside of me, legs danglin' against the sacks. But that time when I looked at him he laughed—laughed all through fit to kill himself, same as I'd been doin'. And it was at himself, y'u know, as well as at the whole thing; he included himself in the show.

"You're quite right," says he.

That was what made y'u love Edmund. When a thing like Washington, D.C., came up, he'd most always get it wrong first—see the bad side of it too big and the good side too small—he had a heap of misplaced seriousness in his system to conquer. But he'd sure conquer it every time if y'u gave him time. It took me the whole first week I worked for him in the store to find this out. Edmund was the squarest man I have ever known. Too square. And about the finest. He was from an Eastern college and entirely wasted on the Thowmet Valley, where nobody but him had any education or understood honesty as he understood it.

"But they're obstacles to the public good here, all the same," said he next; and I had to think back before I saw he meant the old men was obstructin' the school-house and thereby withholdin' light from the young hope of the great empire of the Northwest.

He came back to it, too, several days after that, while the school-teacher was orderin' slate-pencils.

"Oh, leave them alone," says she. "Mr. Edmund, you'll just make 'em worse."

But he was in for an argument. He settled those eyes of his on her with his regular May-God-have-mercy-on-your-soul expression, and he told her she'd ought to know better. But she didn't mind him any more'n I did. She liked him.

"You know as well as I do," says he, "that children should be an improvement on their parents especially when those parents come from Texas. Texas is a large place," he goes on, "and I am willin' to believe that it contains thousands of enlightened and refined persons—but they don't come here. If your scholars don't learn to read and write, where's any progress to come from?"

"Well, Mr. Edmund," says she, "all I know is that you will never help me, or the school-

house, or progress, by calling Kultus Jake
and Frisco Baldy a pair of inspected and con-
demned mules to their faces.''

I didn't know he'd called 'em that. Must
have been outside the store somewheres. Edmund could turn his tongue wrong-side-out
when he felt like it. ''That's what they are,''
says he, laughin' at his own words, which he
had forgotten. ''But as for this valley, it was
inhabited by better citizens when the wild animals lived here. I prefer a black-tailed deer
to a Texan. Don't waste your money on those
chocolates, Miss Carey.''

''Why, what's wrong with them?'' says
she with the box in her hand.

''There's no chocolate in 'em,'' says Edmund. ''The wholesale house cheated me. I'd
send 'em back, but I'd sold too much before
I found out. This candy here,'' says he, show-
in' her some more, ''seems to be what it
claims to be.''

And then, while she seemed to hesitate over
the chocolates, what do y'u suppose he does?
Takes the box sudden out of her hand, walks
out to the river bank and throws the whole
outfit plop into the water!

''Isn't that just like him!'' says she to me,
very quiet, while he was out on the bank. And

it was. Yes, Edmund is the only fool I ever loved.

She kept starin' out at him, and in a minute we heard the noise of a boat bein' rowed acrost the Thowmet. Edmund he stands watchin' whoever it was below. Next minute up the bank comes Kultus Jake.

"No use your divin' for that candy," says Edmund; "it's all melted by now."

But Jake didn't know about the candy and he had somethin' on his mind. His old innocent blue eyes was troubled.

"Decided where Washington, D.C., is?" says Edmund, walkin' ahead of him into the store.

But that didn't faze Jake; he'd come to say somethin'. I thought Washington, D.C., was a thing of the past. As a matter of fact it hadn't scarcely begun; it was bidin' its time for all of us, though none of us could ever suspect that.

"Well, where's your partner this afternoon?" says Edmund.

Kultus Jake he walks around the store blinkin' at the various goods, and he touches a trap here and a blanket there and after a while he answers:—

"Oh, he's over to Pipestone Cañon." And

he walks around and touches some more goods.

"Figure you'll get into the mountains this season?" says Edmund.

"Yes," says Jake. "Next week." Then he walks up close to Edmund. "Baldy's over to Pipestone Cañon," says he. "We're goin' to start next week. Don't want the snow to get ahead of us. Mink and marten reported plentiful up Robinson Creek. One man seen a silver-gray fox. Guess we'll do pretty well this winter. Live in Robinson Cabin—it ain't fallen down like they claimed." And he took another turn around by the door. Well, all this wasn't much to tell people. We knowed all that ourselves—but Jake just then made up his mind quick to say what he'd come to say.

"Don't you josh Baldy," says he, comin' back close up to Edmund. "Don't you do it any more. I don't mind joshin', but Baldy—he's old."

And out he goes. He went down the bank, and next y'u could hear the knockin' of his oars, as he rowed himself back over the Thowmet to their tent. Miss Carey she looked at the door where he'd gone out, smilin' very pretty. It takes a woman to understand them feelin's men has, but conceals.

"Well, I must be getting home for supper,"
says she. She boarded a little ways up the
North Fork with some folks that had quite
a family. But when she's outside, just startin'
to untie her horse, "Why, here comes Frisco
Baldy!" says she, and waits for him.

Frisco Baldy was comin', sure enough,
ridin' up the river quite slow, and lookin'
acrost at where their tent was in the flat land
this side o' the blacksmith's cabin. Then we
knowed Jake had spied him and that was
what made him speak out so quick.

Baldy he arrives and gets down. "Been
over to Pipestone Cañon," says he. "We'll
be startin' for the Robinson Cabin next week,
I guess. Snow's not meltin' on the mountain
tops any more. She's liable to come down
here for keeps any day. Well—we'll be
needin' a lot o' truck off you. Beans and pork
and coffee, and stuff in general—me and
Jake'll be over to see you about it. Guess
you'll have to let us pay you in furs when we
come out in the spring. Old man Parrigin
seen a silver-gray fox. Say!" And Baldy
walks clost up to Edmund. "Don't you josh
Jake. He's old."

And out he goes!

I looks at Miss Carey—just in time to catch

her whippin' her handkerchief away from her eye.

"Well," begins Edmund—but she bursts right out on him.

"Don't you say anything! Don't say a thing!" she cries. "They're just two poor, quaint, dear, helpless old waifs." Oh, she looked at Edmund perfectly ragin'.

I didn't know what Edmund would do about that. He had an awful quick temper. But he gives a smile pretty near as lovely as hern had been, and his solemn brown eyes merely looked kind o' surprised.

"Why," says he, "I was goin' to say I would grubstake 'em for nothin'. They needn't give me any furs."

It pulled her right up short and I don't know what she would have said, for there was Frisco Baldy on the bank, hollerin' and throwin' his arms up and down. I run out. I thought somebody was in trouble. Just in the bend there below where the North Fork comes in, there's a big deep hole. Well, no-body was in no trouble. Jake was rowin' himself over to our side again, and Baldy appeared not to want him over on our side. So he kept a-bellerin' and throwin' his arms, and Jake he came along over, not mindin'

about Baldy on the bank. He landed and
clumb up the bank right past Baldy, and
Baldy he yells out:—

"Didn't y'u see me tellin' y'u to stay over
there?"

"Yes, I seen y'u and I come," says Jake, not
yellin', but in his nat'ral voice. And he starts
past him.

"Didn't y'u see I've got the horse and can
cross at the ford without y'u?"

That starts Jake and he yells back: "I
didn't come for you; I came for a box of
matches, y'u bawlin' bobcat."

So there they was at it again, scrappin'
about nothin' at all. And Jake he bought his
matches, mad, and cleared out to his boat;
and old Baldy he got on his horse, mad, and
cleared out to the ford; and I don't know,
when they got to their tent, whether they
went on with that partic'lar dissension or
whether they'd forgot all about it and had to
start up a new one to keep 'em from feelin'
lost. Oh, they'd contracted the habit o' dis-
agreement, I suppose, same as a man gets to
depend on havin' a quid of tobacco in his
cheek. But while speakin' to Edmund about
his joshin', the eyes of both of 'em had given
away the store they set by each other.

Miss Carey she went home with her slate-pencils ordered and some candy Edmund's conscience was willin' for him to recommend, and me and Edmund was left alone in the store. I wanted to say somethin' about Kultus Jake and Frisco Baldy's latest unpleasantness, and somethin' about the way each one had sneaked in to ask Edmund not to josh the other one any more; and I had things to say about the bad chocolates, and about Edmund's plan of grubstakin' the old junipers when they should start into the mountains for a winter's trappin'—I was full of conversation, but Edmund wasn't. He was loaded plumb to the gills with silence. I could tell that from his looks. I had come to know by hard experience that there was spells when Edmund not only didn't want to say a word himself, but didn't want you to, either. And if y'u happened to say anythin'—don't care what—he'd fly at y'u. I said wunst it was goin' to rain, and just merely this started Edmund roundin' me up for the inattentive way I had of lettin' my mind wander from my business. It did rain, too. So now I wondered for a while what he'd say when he felt like speakin' once more. It was generally some very peculiar remark y'u couldn't foresee. Of course Edmund was college-raised, but it wasn't no college-raisin' made him Edmund. I've saw heaps of graduates and undergraduates and they're just like other people when y'u come to know 'em. But I'd forgot wonderin' by the time Edmund did speak. He made me jump.

"I am the oldest man in this valley."

That is what he said in the store long after dark with two lamps. He was makin' out an order to send to Seattle by the mail next day —a big order, because it was likely to be the last lot of goods we could send for that year. Freight teams couldn't get into the valley after the heavy snow came.

Well, I didn't say anythin', for I wasn't full of conversation any more. Edmund he stands back of his desk and shoves his spectacles up on his forehead, and his eyes was lookin' at me so y'u'd have thought I'd committed— well, most anythin'.

"Very much the oldest man in this valley," says Edmund, lookin' more serious—if possible.

"All right," says I.

"I will be twenty-five," says Edmund, "next fourteenth of July. I'm going to bed."

So he marched out with his lamp and left

me in the store with all the shadows and
things, and the sound of the North Fork
rapids under the bridge. One lamp made awful little light in that store. D'y'u think I
laughed at Edmund then, like I so often did?
Not a bit. I sat down on the counter and
thought him over. And for the first time I
expect I saw him clear. Saw him alone in that
valley, unlike anybody or anythin' that was
there, or likely to come there. And him with
his college mates and all men and women who
set store by him miles and miles and miles
away in the East. It made me feel old and
lonesome myself! And then—throwin' those
chocolates into the river! Maybe he was the
oldest man in the valley, for Jake and Baldy
had crossed the line into childhood.

But I laughed at him next mornin'. The
Siwash had started down the valley with the
mail and no one had come to the store yet that
early—it was dark. So Edmund had nothin'
to do, and he was weighin' himself on the
scales.

"I don't gain," says he, disgusted. "Not a
pound in a year."

"Y'u don't think the thoughts that make a
man fat," says I.

"A hundred and forty," says he, and
jumps down.

Well, I did weigh a hundred and sixty,
stripped, right along—and we was pretty
near of a height. Maybe I had half an inch
the better of him. "But," I tells him for consolation, "it's your great age. You'll be
twenty-five next July and I was only twenty-
four last June." It was November we was in,
y'u know. So I laughs.

"Yes!" he says. "You twenty-four! You
stopped maturing at six." And he laughs, too.

The Siwash was late comin' back with the
mail over the Chillowisp. Snow must have
been three foot deep in the mountains, and it
lay for quite a while in the valley, so we
thought Kultus Jake and Frisco Baldy had
waited too late and would lose their chance
to get to their trappin'. They did lose it, too,
but not exactly that way—but I'll come to
that point when I get there. Snow druv school
indoors. Miss Carey she had to quit the tent
—and sure enough it turned out like I told
y'u. Edmund's sittin'-room was filled up with
Texan kids—Edmund's private room, which
he had so nicely fixed up with all his college
things: mugs, flags, an oar, pictures of his
friends, a whole heap of stuff. It had to be
used for the school, bein' the only possible
place, or school had to stop till spring come
round and the tent could serve again. Well,

Edmund wasn't willin' to cut off the hope of
the empire of the Northwest for five whole
months. Of course they wasn't there Satur-
days and Sundays, or at night, or at hours
when he really needed his room—he was in
the store durin' school-time—but every day,
after the kids had gone home, poor Edmund
he had to open all the windows of his pet
room. He caught Miss Carey sweepin' it of
their leavin's and scolded her savage for that.
Insisted on sweepin' it himself. Would have
his way. My sakes, but he was a cross man
every day while he was sweepin'! Then the
kids they bruck one or two of his souvenirs,
touchin' and meddlin' with them, and Miss
Carey was wild. Edmund didn't mind half as
much. She spoke to me as we was takin' a
ride together one Sunday, when the snow had
melted most off again. Guess it was early in
December. She wanted her folks back in
Orange, New Jersey, to buy new things and
send 'em out. She was earnest about it. She
was a nice-lookin' girl. I remember that ride.
Tamaracks was all yello' and sheddin',
makin' yello' patches on the snow with their
needles, but the pines was that green they
was black a little ways off, and the wind smelt
of 'em strong.

"I wanted particularly to replace the glass decanter," she says, "but it only made him rude to me. I had to tell him it was a very strange thing that the only gentleman in the valley should be the one person who had been rude."

"Goodness to gracious!" I shouts out, "what did he say?"

"That I was the only lady in the valley, and that explained it."

"Well," I says, "he's never apologized as handsome as that to me." So we both laughs.

"But," she says just before we got home, "he ought not to tease those poor old men."

"Well, he's not done it lately—not in my hearin'," I says.

It happened Edmund had done it. Couldn't keep his mouth shut about the school-house question. It was the old men's duty, he claimed, to give their land for the school-house. Edmund was awful about people's duty. He brung it up, though, in a new way. He thought he was makin' a joke. Hands out the pieces of the decanter to Jake and Baldy, and tells 'em they done that damage and it was their business to make it good; so when they, who had never seen the decanter before, didn't make out what he was drivin' at,

Edmund tells 'em they're the final cause. He explains how if they'd given their land, the school-house would have been built and no accidents would have occurred. Edmund meant that to be funny, but Jake and Baldy went off cursin' him and the school and the whole valley, and wasn't a bit grateful for learnin' what a final cause is.

But back they comes in a day or two as usual, as if no words had passed, and they buy their truck to go trappin'. Takes 'em all day, but Edmund is wonderful patient. So they can't start that day. So they comes back next day to pack up and start. And it was then that Washington, D.C., comes up again. The Siwash was a day overdue with the mail, and some of the Texans was assembled at the store to see the mail arrive. They expected no letters, but it was somethin' to do and they always done it—assembled and stood around inside the store and out. Then to-day they had more to do, for there was Kultus Jake and Frisco Baldy and their horses, packin' up their stuff. That gave everybody a chance to make remarks and be wise. They hardly noticed the mail when it did come about ten o'clock, they was so busy tellin' the old men the best way to do every-

thin'—best trap, best bait, best way to make
a set—when Edmund he begins to lecture. He
comes out with a letter in his hand and holds
it up. That's the subject of the lecture. Letter
has come to the wrong Beekman. It was
mailed at Portland, Awregon, and addressed
to "Beekman, Massachusetts," and it has
come out of its way to "Beekman, Washington," thereby losin' a lot of time, of course.
For it had went over the Northern Pacific on
its right way as far as Spokane, and then had
come back through Coulee City away up here,
and it would get to Beekman, Massachusetts,
about two weeks late.

"It all comes," says Edmund, "of havin'
places of the same name. That ought to be
against the law." He told us there was nine
Beekmans. He took it to heart heavy, as
usual. "As the country grows and settles
up," he says, "they'll keep on namin' places
Beekman. There'll be a hundred Beekmans
before we're through. It ought to be a state's
prison offence."

"In that case," says a Texas parent, "you
couldn't call this territory Washington."

"I guess this is a free country," says another.

"I guess," says another, "the folks that

live in a place has the right to call that place
what they see fit.''

Poor Edmund! It wasn't no use him ex-
plainin' the confusion it made.

''There's forty-eight places named Washington now,'' says he. ''I've looked it up.
There ought to be just one. The capital of the
United States. And the map is pitted with
'em like smallpox.''

''Washington, D. C., Maryland,'' says
Frisco Baldy, haulin' in slack on the diamond
hitch.

''Virginia,'' says Kultus Jake, on the other
side of the pack.

Edmund he just give 'em both a witherin'
look, and he whirls back into the store and
gets to work at his desk. Wouldn't come out
to tell the old men good-by when they started
off up the river, although he was grubstakin'
'em for nothin'. They didn't know that, of
course. Expected to pay him in furs when
they come back in the spring.

''You'll not get very far to-day,'' says an
onlooker to the departin' junipers. ''You're
makin' a late start.''

''Camp at Early Winter,'' one of 'em says.
Early Winter was a creek that come into the
main stream about halfway to the Robinson
Cabin.

"Wake la-le hyas cole snass," says the Siwash mail-carrier.

"Oh, no, it ain't," says a Texan, lookin' the weather up and down.

"Well, I think maybe it will," says another, sweepin' his eyes around the sky. "And maybe it won't."

So that sets 'em discussin' the probabilities of a big snow and if Siwashes knowed about such things more'n white men did. They concluded Siwashes was inferior to white men in every respect, and it wasn't goin' to snow.

"Good luck!" one of 'em calls out. But Kultus Jake and Frisco Baldy was by that time on the bridge over the North Fork, and couldn't hear him.

No more events took place that day. The kids finished their school and went home. Miss Carey she went home. Edmund opened the windows and swept the floor. A few folks bought things durin' the day, or came to buy and didn't, and some had letters to go out next day. There was always a little more hustle round mailtimes. But a lonesome winter softness filled the valley and seemed to make y'u hear the stove plainer. The trunks of the trees kind of appeared more silent. Everythin' was quieter. I remember Edmund looked out of the door about sundown and

said the Siwash had been right, there was
goin' to be a big snow. Even his voice sounded
quieter in the clouded-over light, and Edmund's voice was always deep—the voice of a
man who was all man. Lyin' in bed that night
I never knowed the dark could be so still.
Funny thing was, I heard the rapids under the
bridge all of a sudden. Of course they'd been
goin' right on all the time. What makes y'u
notice things and not notice 'em? It got very
solemn, that room did, in the dark. Those old
men was too old to go off into the mountains.
Then I heard the little sound of the snowflakes
around on the cabin. They must have started
fallin' pretty late, for next mornin' it wasn't
deep, not four inches yet, but it was keepin'
on. Old man Parrigin come in about nine, and
he says he had told everybody yesterday a
storm was comin'. As a matter of fact, he'd
been one of the surest no storm was comin'.
It made Edmund look sour at him. And bye
and bye another prophet drops in, and he
says he had offered to bet it would snow. And
by eleven o'clock the fifth Texan had come
along to sit around the stove; and he says—
like every one of 'em had done before him—
that anybody could have told it was goin' to
snow. Oh, not one of 'em had ever doubted

it for a minute! It gets too much for Edmund
to bear, and he pushes up his spectacles high
on his forehead and looks at me, mournful
as anythin'.

"Last Fourth of July," says he to me, "I
said it was going to snow to-day."

Old man Parrigin he starts laughin' at that.
He come from New York State and he could
see a joke, even when Edmund made it. But
when y'u make that kind of a joke to a Texan
—the kind of Texan that moves away from
Texas—he says you're insultin' him. Around
the stove they all looks dignified and spits
without words. We could hear the rapids, and
indoors the kids was singin' some kind of
Christmas chorus Miss Carey was teachin'
to 'em. Their voices come to us through a
couple of shut doors. One of the Texans as
had been insulted by Edmund's joke now
asserts his self-respect by changin' the subject.

"Washington, D.C.," says he, "is in Pennsylvania."

Edmund he sighs heavy and goes on postin'
up his ledger.

Old man Parrigin gives me a nudge. "I
wonder if Miss Carey would hold a night-
school?" says he, and winks.

The fellars around the stove they spits
some more. They was afraid. That's what
was the matter. Plain it was there had been
talk among 'em, ridin' away yesterday after
Edmund's remarks. Maybe some of 'em
knowed their geography correct on that point,
but they didn't feel they knowed it correct
enough to insist upon it in the presence of
witnesses. Anyway they drops it now, and
after some further spittin' they changes the
subject again.

"There'll be plenty snow at the Robinson
Cabin," says one.

"Plenty at Early Winter by now," another
says.

"Oh, they'll get through," says a third.

"I wonder if they'll get my silver-gray
fox," says old man Parrigin. So the talk
turns for a while on trappin', and dies down
till the rapids was the only noise; and then a
Texan got up and stretched himself, and said
he'd be late for dinner, he guessed, if he
didn't begin to think some about startin'
home. So he began to think, I suppose, though
it didn't show none on his face. Edmund kep'
a-writin' up his ledger. Y'u could hear the
rapids just as if they had come clost up outside. And the snow was fallin' and fallin'.

Old man Parrigin holds up his hand. "What's that?" he says. So we all pricks up our ears.

The snow had the valley pretty well muffled, but there did seem to be somethin'. So a feller looks out and he says it's somebody comin' acrost the bridge. Hard to tell who it was for the snow. But next minute he got nearer, and it was Frisco Baldy, walkin' his horse turrable slow.

"My God!" says somebody, "somethin's happened." And we all crowds out.

"More horses on the bridge," says Parrigin.

We could all see 'em. It was packhorses creepin' along. Behind 'em trailed a man ridin', and that was Kultus Jake.

"Then what has happened?" somebody says.

Baldy he arrives first, snow on his hat two inches deep. He gets down and jumps some to shake off the snow, and then walks in through us and goes to the stove and takes a chair. Not a word said. Packhorses they arrives and stands around all over snow—stands sad and hang-dog, like they was guilty and had gave up denyin' it. Jake comes along a mile an hour, same as Baldy; and he gets down and

jumps the snow off, and same as Baldy, he
passes through us and goes to the stove. But
he puts it between him and Baldy. Sits down
and don't look at Baldy. So we all comes back
in and sits down, too—except Edmund. He
goes behind his desk and stands up there with
his spectacles pushed high.

"Well?" he says.

Baldy's lips move, but nothin' sounds.

"Well?" Edmund repeats. "Was the trail
snowed up? Anybody dead?"

Jake clears his throat, but that's all.

Then Baldy manages to talk. "No," he
says, kind of croakin'; "trail wasn't snowed
up."

"Not then, it wasn't," says Jake. "Nobody's dead."

Up flares Edmund's temper. He swings a
big hammer down on the counter with a bang,
and he lets out one swear as thorough and
bad as any Western man. Y'u'd been scared
yourself if he'd aimed it at you. After all,
Edmund had grubstaked 'em, though they
didn't know it.

The hammer and the oath dislodge Jake's
voice. "That man," says he, noddin' con-
temptuous acrost the stove at Baldy—"that
man claims it's in Maryland."

I have explained to y'u that Edmund was
an unexpected person in his ways. I looked
for more hammer and more blasphemy. They
had let Washington, D.C., break up their winter's trappin'. But Edmund he slowly relaxes
on the hammer, and he just stands and stands
and keeps a-lookin' at 'em, merely inter-ested
—more and more inter-ested. And they sits
blinkin' at him. Won't look at each other.

Then a Texan speaks. "I have said right
along that it was in Pennsylvania."

There's times when things get altogether
beyond any daily feelin's a man commonly
has. I didn't want to lay down on the flour
sacks this time. Didn't want to laugh at all.
And Edmund wasn't a bit mad. Even old man
Parrigin makes no symptoms except of further inquiry. And the Texans, of course, was
merely anxious to have a point settled that
some of 'em had been disputin' over.

"I wish you would tell me all about it," says
Edmund. Violets ain't milder than he was.

Well, that was exactly what they couldn't
do, y'u see. When they first come in and saw
how we was all anxious over watchin' 'em
arrive I expect it came home to 'em, I expect
it shamed 'em. They took in then the way
they and their actions would look to the

valley, and talkin' came hard to 'em. But once
they got started, they was soon screechin' at
each other as usual, and forgot appearances.
They had got to Early Winter, they had
camped at Early Winter, but on the way there
the argument had come up. Must have growed
pretty warm by bedtime, for it had lasted
through their sleep so they wasn't speakin'
to each other at breakfast. Y'u see, alone up
there with the snow there wasn't nothin' new
to change the subject for 'em. It stayed right
with 'em, and after breakfast it bruck out
worse than ever, Jake for Virginia and Baldy
for Maryland, and they had it all the time
they was packin', givin' each other proofs
where it was; and when they was ready to go
they wouldn't live with each other any more,
wouldn't camp, wouldn't trap, wouldn't speak
—and so they had come home!

So there they was, and there we was, and
there it was. They'd simmered down again
now, after tearin' loose and tellin' all about it.
They was quiet. They sat with the stove between 'em and just blinked on and on. Snow
fallin'; rapids soundin'; nothin' else durin'
it must have been all of a minute—and it felt
like ten.

The strain got too severe for that Texan,

and he spoke with the gentlest, anxiousest
voice, like a child pleadin' for somethin':—

"Say, ain't it in Pennsylvania?"

And outside in the snow one o' them horses
gives a long, weary, hungry neigh.

That horse breakin' in bust somethin' inside of me and Parrigin and Edmund. Edmund he gives a kind of youp! Parrigin curls
over on the counter, and I'd have laid right
down on the sacks, only I wasn't near 'em,
and so I leaned up against the shelves. Nobody else did nothin' because Jake and Baldy
hadn't any heart left after seein' themselves
in their true light, and the other Texans they
was bein' very careful now about their geography—they were savin' it up, they wasn't
givin' any of it away, not even to charity.

But after his youp Edmund pulls himself
up and he takes charge of the meetin', and
when me and Parrigin hears him beginnin' a
speech we comes to and listens.

"This is a great valley," says Edmund, behind his desk. "It has song and story
whipped to a finish." Then he fixes his big
glum eyes on Kultus Jake and Frisco Baldy.
"Don't think," says he, "you'll draw me into
your argument. But you hold the record.
Wherever Washington is, it would have

stayed there till spring. Your words haven't
moved it anywhere else. But you have lost
your winter over this. Couldn't you have
waited and come home with your load of furs,
and been a success instead of a failure? For
you can't turn around and go back into the
mountains now; you'd never get halfway, and
unless unusual weather follows this soon, the
passes will be choked for the next three
months."

Edmund stops with that. It was fairly hard
on the poor old blinkin' junipers—but y'u'll
notice Edmund hadn't told 'em a word about
the grubstakin'. "If everybody will come in
here," he says, "perhaps we can find some
child to settle the question."

He opens the door and we all shambles in
through after him to the school-room. Miss
Carey she rises from her chair, and of course
she don't know what to make of it.

"Miss Carey," says Edmund, "will some
of your scholars kindly tell us what the capital of the United States is, and where it is?"

Miss Carey she looks at the kids sittin'
around the table fixed for 'em. Gosh, y'u'd
ought to have seen the hands fly up all over
the room!

"Everybody may answer," says Miss
Carey.

And out they yells it. It was like the chorus they was practisin' for Christmas.

There was long breaths of relief drawn among the men standin' sheepish by the door —two or three regular sighs come out from that crowd.

"Thank you, Miss Carey," says Edmund, "and please excuse us for troubling you." So he leads the way back into the store and goes behind his desk. If anybody expected him to make another speech they was disappointed. Edmund looked cold and ca'm, and just as unconcerned as though he'd been addin' sums or readin' a two-weeks-old newspaper. He starts writin' at his ledger.

"Well, I'll be late for dinner," says the Texan.

"I told y'u where it was," says another.

One by one they shuffles out, Jake and Baldy mixed in with them, and they swings up on to their horses and slowly goes away— up the river and down the river and acrost the bridge—till y'u could see none of 'em no more through the fallin' snow; and in the store was just Edmund writin', and me lookin' at him, and the sound of the rapids.

Did Edmund talk then? That wouldn't have been Edmund. Nothin' was said in that store by him or me for—well, it must have been

quite a while before the door opened and Miss
Carey she pokes her head in and wants to
know if she may be so bold as to inquire what
all that meant in the school-room. The kids
had gone home early for fear of the snow.
So Edmund he smiles perfectly peaceful and
tells her about it. So, of course, she thinks
it very comic and she laughs hearty—but all of
a sudden she remembers and expresses sympathy for Edmund's misplaced generosity.

"Don't let that trouble you," says he, gay
enough. "I meant to grubstake 'em, and I
will. It shall not cost 'em a cent. Don't tell
the poor old idiots."

So that was that. But the poor old idiots
had somethin' more to say. They had a
thought. It snowed away all that night—a
great big snow—but next mornin' it had quit
and there was promise of its turnin' into a fine
large day. The kids had come to school pretty
late, but they come. And then into the store
walks Kultus Jake and Frisco Baldy. For a
while they walks around and just inspects all
the goods they knowed by heart anyway.

"Well?" says Edmund. And they looks at
each other.

"Could we step into the school-room just a
minute?" says Jake then.

Edmund he looks surprised, but asks no

questions, and in we all goes. Miss Carey she gets up again.

"Any more information?" says she, pleasant.

"No," says Jake.

"Not to-day," says Baldy.

"We," says Jake, "well—we—we'd—"

Baldy gets restless and he steps up. "Put your school-house on our land," says he.

"We want to give it to y'u," says Baldy.

"Coal and all," says Jake.

There was a pink color went over Miss Carey's face—all over it—and she didn't say a word for a while; she looks quick at Edmund and then she looks back at the two old men, and her eyes has tears in 'em.

"Folks ought to know geography," says Jake.

"We want the kids in this valley to know it," says Baldy.

"Knowledge will save 'em from mistakes," says Jake.

And then Miss Carey she speaks at last. "Thank you," she says.

"Is this *potlatch?*" inquires Edmund, jokin'.

"*Kultus potlatch!*" says both of 'em together.

The school-house was built in the spring;

and after the school got into it, now and again
Jake and Baldy would sneak up to the door,
look in and take a back seat. And one of 'em
would say he'd like to ask the kids a question:
Where was Washington, D.C.? And when the
answer came, Jake and Baldy they'd laugh
like they'd split and sneak out again.

But d'you suppose not havin' Washington
to scrap about left 'em peaceable? Not it.
They lit on some new cause for scrappin'
most every day. You could hear 'em at it. Up
to the last. One day in the store we heard the
knockin' sound of a boat bein' rowed over the
river, and Baldy came into the store alone.
He walks to Edmund, but he looks down on
the floor.

"Jake's sick," says he. "Jake's sick."

There was no doctor in the valley, but what
could a doctor do? In about three days we
had Baldy sick, too. The tie between 'em was
the tie of life, and Jake died of a Saturday
and Baldy died Monday.

"They must be buried by the school-
house," says Miss Carey. And everybody
went. And then up comes the question what
to put on the headboard? It brought up something none of us had thought of.

"Why, we don't even know their names!"
says Miss Carey, very soft.

We didn't know anything. They had come into the valley, they had made the valley laugh, they were gone. That was all. Not a fact or a birthplace or anythin' to put over them that would tell who they had been. But Miss Carey wasn't goin' to let it be like that. She took it in charge and she got it right. She found a bit of poetry and she had the board painted, and it was this way: "Jake and Baldy. Our Friends. Their heart was free from malice, and all their anger was excess of love."

That was slush, of course. Excess of love between them two old junipers? Not it. They was just used to each other. Couldn't get along alone. Of course they had decent points. 'Most any man has. I have. Bet you have.

And then along in July Edmund got married to Miss Carey. They was sure a happy two!

"Are y'u still the oldest man in the valley?" I asks Edmund one day in the store.

"About three and a half," says Edmund, solemn and deep. But then he laughs.

Oh, yes, their happiness filled that store, filled the whole cabin, crowded it. Maybe that's why I left the valley.

VIII

THE DRAKE WHO HAD MEANS OF HIS OWN

SCIPIO sat beside the table—Mrs. Culloden's still very new, wedding-present table—arguing on and on, and I forgot all about him. When he slapped the Wyoming game laws for that year down on the table hard, and complained that I was not listening to him, I continued to look out of the ranch window at the pond and merely said:—

"Just hear those ducks."

He stared at me with disgust and scorn. "Ducks!" he then muttered.

"Well, but hear them," I urged.

"Well, they're quackin'," he said. "A duck does." He picked up the game laws and resumed: "As I was telling you, it says—page 12, section 25—"

But I gave him no attention and still looked out at the pond.

So then he remarked bitterly: "I suppose ducks crow back East—or bark."

He was perfectly welcome to all the satire he could invent; I was not to be turned from my curiosity about the clamor in the water outside, and as I watched I said aloud: "There's something behind it."

This brought him to the window, where, as he stood silent beside me, I could feel his impatience as definitely as if it had been a radiator. The matter was that he had his mind running on something and I had my mind running on something—and they weren't the same things; and each of us wished the other to be interested in his own thing.

"Something behind it," echoed Scipio slightingly. "Behind every quack you'll find a duck."

To this I returned no answer.

"Maybe they have forgot themselves and laid eggs in the water," suggested Scipio.

"Do your Western ducks lay much in September?" I inquired, with chill.

The noise in the pond, which had died down for an instant, was now set up again—loud, remonstrant, voluble; the two birds sat in the middle of the water and lifted up their heads and screamed to the sky.

"That's what they've done," said Scipio; "and they can't locate the eggs. Well, it'd make me holler, too. Say," he pleaded, "what's the point in your point, anyhow? I want to show you about those game laws."

"Must I hear it all over again and must I say it all over again?" I responded, not taking my eye from the pond.

"You've never heard it wunst yet, for you've never listened."

"I did. I didn't begin to wander till you began repeating the whole thing for the third time. And now I'll say for the fourth time, it's a closed season till 1912. There they go out of the pond, single file—Duchess in the lead. The Duchess has purple in her wings; the Countess has none."

"Oh, soap fat!" said Scipio.

"And they've gone to feed on the grain in the haystack. There's Sir Francis waiting for them by the woodpile. He's the drake."

"Oh, soap fat!" repeated Scipio.

I followed the ducks until they had waddled out of sight.

"Every now and then, during the day," I said, "they go through that same performance: sit in the water and scream louder each minute, then come out and head for the haystack in the most orderly, quiet manner, just after having given every symptom of falling into convulsions. Now I'm going to find out what that means. And what I am wondering at," I continued, "is why you do not suggest that they are screaming at the game laws."

Well, we sat down then and had it out about those game laws; and it is but right to confess that they were more important to poor Scipio than the ducks were to me. First we took section 25 to pieces, dug its sentences to the bottom, and carefully lifted out every scrap which gave promise of containing sense. It was no child's task. You didn't reach the first full stop for a hundred and twelve words—nothing but commas; it was like being lost in the sage-brush—and, by the time the full stop did come, your head—but let me quote the sentence:—

"It shall be unlawful for any person or persons to kill any antelope until the open season for other game animals in 1915, when only one antelope may be killed by any person hunting legally, or to kill any moose, elk or mountain sheep until the open season for other game animals, in 1912, when only one male moose may be killed by any person hunting legally, or to kill any elk or mountain sheep in any part of this state, except in Fremont County, Uinta County, Carbon County and that part of Bighorn County and Park County west of the Bighorn River, until the open season for game animals in 1915."

To tell you all that we said before we had finished with this would be worse than useless—it would be profane; enough that I stuck to the conclusion I had reached when I read the section in the East—no hunting anything anywhere for anybody until 1912. On the strength of it I had left my rifle at home and brought only my fishing rod.

"If it is your way," said Scipio, "what do you make of section 26? 'It shall be unlawful for any person or persons to hunt, pursue or kill any elk, deer or mountain sheep except from September twenty-fifth to November thirtieth of *each year*.'" He yelled the last two words at me.

But I merely clapped my hands to my brow.

"And if it is your way," Scipio pursued, playing his ace, "what do you make of Honey Wiggin taking a party out next Monday for six weeks?"

"Why, they'll simply all be arrested."

"No; they'll not. I saw Honey's license with this year stamped in red figures right acrost it, just as plain as headlines."

What could one reply to that? I picked up the pamphlet and stared at the page.

Scipio ruminated. "Will you tell me," he said, "why, in a country where everybody's born equal, the legislature should be a bigger fool than anybody else?"

"It's a free country," I reminded him. "Every man has the right to be an ass here."

But Scipio still brooded. "Well," he said, "if I was a legislator—" he stopped.

"You're not qualified," said I.

"Not?"

"You haven't sufficient command of the English language."

"*What!*" cried Scipio; for vocabulary is his chief pride and I had actually touched him.

"No. You couldn't cook up two paragraphs of your mother tongue that would defy any sane human intelligence."

"They have done worse than that to me," he said ruefully. "They have lost me my season's job. The party I was to take out read them laws same as you did, and they stayed back East and made other plans. That's what I got in last night's mail."

"Well, I haven't stayed back East," I said. "The fishing's about done, but I want an excuse for another month or two of outing. My things can get here in twelve days—we'll hunt, and I'll be your season's job. And," I added, "now I shall have time to study the ducks."

We launched then into discussion of horses

and camp outfit, copiously arguing what the
legislature would let a man hunt, pursue, or
kill in a season it declared to be open for no
big game at all, until from eleven the clock
went round to noon; and in the kitchen the
voice of Mrs. Culloden was heard, calling
clearly to her young bridegroom in the corral
—calling too clearly.

"Well, Jimsy," the voice said, "are you
going to get me any wood for this stove—or
ain't you?"

Our discussion dropped; we sat still; it was
time for Scipio to be getting back across the
river to his own cabin and dinner. He rose,
put on his hat, and stood looking at me for
a moment. Then he took his hat off and
scratched his head, glancing toward the kitchen.

"Jimsy, did you hear me telling you about
that wood?" came the voice of the young
bride, a trifle clearer. "I seem to have to
remind you of everything."

Scipio's bleached blue eye and his long, ec-
centric nose turned slowly once more on me.
"My, but it's turrable easy to get married,"
was his word. He shoved his hat on again
and was out of the door and on his horse;
and I watched him ride down to the river

and ford it. As he grew distant, my three
ducks waddled back from the haystack to the
pond. The Duchess led, the Countess followed; Sir Francis brought up the rear. But
how could I attend to them while the following reached me through the door from the
kitchen?

"If dinner's late you can thank yourself,
Jimsy."

"Why, May, I split the wood for you right
after breakfast. That corral gate—"

"Split the wood and leave me to carry it!"

"Well, I've been about as busy as I could
be on the ditch; and that gate needs—"

"Never mind. Wash your hands and get
ready now. Kiss me first."

At this point it seemed best to go out of the
sitting-room door and come presently into
the kitchen by the other way, at the moment
when my hostess was placing the hot food
upon the table. It was good food, well cooked;
and all the spoons and things were bright and
clean. Bright and clean, too, and very pretty,
was the little bride. She was not twenty yet;
Jimsy was not twenty-four; and as he sat
down to his meal I saw her look at him with
a look which I understood plainly: had no
stranger been there to see, some more kissing

would have occurred. Yet, what did she now find to say to him—she that so visibly adored him?

"Jimsy Culloden! Well, I guess you'll never learn to brush your hair!"

Jimsy suddenly grinned. "Others have enjoyed it pretty well this way," said he. "Tangled their hands all through it." And his gray eyes twinkled at me. But the little woman's blue eyes flashed and she sat up very stiff. "Before I asked you, that was," Jimsy added.

Have I ever told you how Jimsy became married? I believe not—but it would take too long now; it will have to wait. His bachelor liveliness had not contributed to his mother's peace of mind, but all was now well; the poker chips had gone I don't know where; our beloved old card-table of past years stood now in the bridal bedroom, stifled in feminine drapery beyond recognition; the bottles that in these days lay empty beyond the corral had contained merely tomato ketchup and such things; and here was Jimsy Culloden a stable citizen, an anchored man, county commissioner, selling vegetables, alfalfa, and horses, with me for a paying boarder in that new-established Wyoming industry which is locally termed dude-wrangling. The eastern "dude" is destined to replace Hereford cattle in Wyoming—and sheep also.

Jimsy was an anchored man, to be sure: might he possibly some day drag his anchor? I glanced at his blue-eyed May, so fair and competent, and I hoped her voice would not grow much clearer. I glanced at Jimsy, quietly eating, and wondered if a new look lately lurking in his eye—a look of slight bewilderment—would increase or pass.

"Didn't I see Scipio Le Moyne ride away?" he asked me.

"Yes. It was dinner-time."

"Couldn't he stay here and eat?"

"There you go, Jimsy Culloden; wanting to feed this whole valley every day, just like you was rich!"

Jimsy's gray eyes blinked and he attended to his plate. The failure of that little joke about tangled hair was the probable cause of his present silence, and the bride appealed to me.

"Ain't that so?" she said. "You've been here before. You know how folks loaf around up and down this valley and stop to dinner, and stay for supper, and just eat people up!"

She was so perfectly right in principle that

my only refuge from the perilous error of taking sides was the somewhat lame remark: "Well, Scipio isn't a dead-beat, you know."

"There!" cried Jimsy, triumphantly.

"Mr. Culloden would have fed a dead-beat just the same," returned the lady promptly.

Again she was entirely right. From good heart and long habit Jimsy made welcome every passing traveler and his horse. When Wyoming was young and its ranches lay wide, desert miles apart, such hospitality was the natural, unwritten law; but now, in this day of increasing settlements and of rainbowed folders of railroads painting a promised land for all comers, a young ranchman could easily be kept poor by the perpetual drain on his groceries and his oats. Jimsy's wife was stepping between him and his bachelor shiftlessness in all directions, and the propitious signs of her influence were everywhere. Indoors and out, a crisp, new appearance of things harbingered good fortune. Why, she had actually started him on reforming his gates! Did you ever see the thing they were frequently satisfied to call a gate in Wyoming? A sordid wreck of barbed wire and rotten wood, hung across the fence-gap by a rusty loop, raggedly dangling like the ribs of a broken umbrella.

The telephone bell called Mrs. Culloden to the sitting-room near the end of dinner.

Mrs. Sedlaw, her dear friend and schoolmate living five miles up the valley, was inviting them to dinner the next day to eat roast grouse.

"Let's go," said Jimsy.

"And you quit your ditch and me quit my ironing?" answered the clear voice. "Thank you ever so much, Susie; we'd just love to, but Jimsy can't go off the ranch this week and I'd not like to leave him all alone, even if I wasn't as busy as I can be with our wash." There followed exchange of gossip and laughter over it, and much love sent to and fro—and the receiver was hung up.

"As for grouse," I said to Jimsy, for his silence was on my nerves, "I will now go and catch you some trout superior to any bird that flies."

Sir Francis, the snow-white drake, stood by the woodpile as I crossed the enclosure on my way to the river. In the pond the lady ducks were loudly quacking, but I passed them by. I desired the solitude of Buffalo Horn, its pools, its cottonwoods, its quiet presiding mountains; and I walked up its stream for a mile, safe from that clear voice and from the bewildered eye of Jimsy, my once blithe, careless friend.

Unless it be from respect for Izaak Walton and tradition, I know not why I ever carry in my fly-book, or ever use, a brown-hackle; it has wasted hours of fishing time for me. The hours this afternoon it did not waste, because, under the spell of the large day that shone upon the valley, my thoughts dwelt not on fish, but with delicious vagueness upon matrimony, the game laws and those ducks. With the waters of Buffalo Horn talking near by and singing far off, I watched all things rather than my line and often wholly stopped to smell the wild, clean odor of the sage-brush and draw the beauty of everything into my very depths. So from pool to pool I waded down the south fork of Buffalo Horn and had caught nothing when I reached Sheep Creek, by Scipio's ranch. Here I changed to a grizzly king and soon had killed four trout.

Scipio was out in his meadow gathering horses, and he came to the bank with a question:—

"Find the eggs them ducks laid in the water?"

"Jimsy wanted to know why you didn't stay to dinner," was my answer.

"Huh!" Scipio watched me land a half-pound fish. Then: "They ain't been married a year yet."

I cast below a sunken log and took a small trout, which I threw back, while Scipio resumed:

"Why I didn't stop to dinner! Huh! Say, when did they quit havin' several wives at wunst?"

"Who quit?"

"Why, them sheep-men back in the Bible—Laban and Solomon and them old-timers. What made 'em quit?"

"They didn't all quit. There, you've made me lose that fish. Are you thinking two wives would be twice as bad as one?"

"You'll get another fish. I'm thinking they wouldn't be half as bad as one."

Certain passages in Scipio's earlier days came into my mind, but I did not mention them to him. Possibly he was thinking of them himself.

"Two at once is not considered moral in this country," I said.

Scipio mused. "I'm not sure I've clearly understood about morals," he muttered. "Are you going to keep that whitefish?"

"I always keep a few for the hens. Mrs. Culloden says it makes 'em lay."

This caused Scipio to look frowningly

across Buffalo Horn to where the Culloden
Ranch buildings lay clear in the blue crystal
of the afternoon light. "Marriage ain't
learned in a day," he remarked, "any more
than ropin' stock is. He ain't learned how to
be married yet."

Again I thought of Scipio's past adven-
tures and remembered that the best critics are
they who have failed in art.

"Did you mean what you said about hunting with me?" Scipio now inquired.

"Sure thing!" I returned, "if you're right
about Honey Wiggin."

"Oh, I'm right enough. You'll see him come
by here Monday."

"Then I'll send East for my things," I
said.

"Well, I'll be looking for a man to cook and
horse-wrangle," said Scipio.

As I approached the ranch across the level
pasture with my fish, I could hear from afar
the quack of the ducks, invisible in the pond,
and could see from afar the snow-white figure
of the drake, stationary by the woodpile. Now
for the first time the idea glimmered upon me
that he had something to do with it. But
what? I came to the breast of the little pond
and stood upon it to watch the Countess and

the Duchess. They were making a great noise; but over what? Sometimes they sat still and screamed together; a punctuation of silence would then follow. Next one or the other would take it up alone. Was it a sort of service they were holding to celebrate the sunset? I looked up at the lustrous crimson on the mountain wall—a mile of giant battlements sending forth a rose glow as if from within, like something in a legend; birds and beasts might well celebrate such a marvel— but the Countess and Duchess were doing this at other hours, when nothing particular seemed to be happening. I looked at the drake by the woodpile. He had not moved a quarter of an inch. He stood in profile, most becomingly. His neat, spotless white, his lemon-colored bill, his orange-colored legs, his benign yet confident attitude, as if of personal achievement taken for granted but not thrust forward—all this put me in mind of something, but so faintly that I could not just then make out what it was. Shouts from the Duchess at the top of her voice hastily recalled my attention to the pond.

I expected to find something sudden was wrong. Not at all. The water was without a wrinkle, the ducks floated motionless: yet there had been a note, a quality, urgent, piercingly remonstrant, in those quacks of the Duchess. She might have been calling for the constabulary, the fire brigade, and the health department. And then, without change for better or for worse in anything around us that I could see, the two birds swam placidly to land. They got out on the bank, wiggled their tails, stood on their toes to flap their wings, and, this brief drying process being over, they took their way to the drake. He stood by the woodpile, stock-still in profile; he had not yet moved a quarter of an inch; it seemed to me —but I was not certain—that his ladies raced as they drew near him. When they reached him he turned with gravity and headed for the haystack. They fell in behind him and the three waddled and wobbled solemnly toward their goal, squeezed under the fence and were lost to view.

I took in my trout to Mrs. Culloden, who praised their size and my skill. On the subject of giving her hens a diet of whitefish, she told me it was her great ambition so to manage that before the moulting fowls should wholly stop laying the spring pullets should have begun to lay.

"Jimsy is real fond of eggs," she explained, "and I want him to have them."

I further learned that whitefish cooked were better than whitefish raw, which often tainted the eggs with a fishy taste. I stood high in the little bride's favor because I was helping her to please Jimsy. Lying abed that night in my one-room cabin, I said aloud, abruptly: "That was a protest."

I know nothing about what they call our subconscious workings, save that I am choke-full of them; I meant the Duchess. Apparently my subconscious works had been dealing with her ever since the scene at the pond. A conclusion had popped out of my mouth full-fledged before I knew it was there. "Yes," I repeated; "she was protesting. They both were."

The works, however, must have stopped after that for the night—or turned to other activity—for next morning I went down to the pond with nothing beyond the two theories of yesterday: that it was protest and that the drake was somehow at the bottom of it. But I scored no advance in my knowledge. All three birds were in the water and did not come out while I remained there; nothing more of their plan of life was revealed to me. Still, I saw one new thing. Sir Francis swam about, with the Duchess and Countess in a suite, following close, but never crowding him. What they did do was crowd each other. A struggle for place occurred between them from time to time; and, although all the rest of the time they were like sisters, when the struggle was on it was bitter.

I must have stayed watching them for half an hour to make sure of this and I know that there were moments when they would have gladly killed each other. Sir Francis never took the slightest notice of it, though he must have been well aware of it, since it always went on some six inches behind his back. The Countess would attempt to swim up closer to him, at which the Duchess would instantly crook her neck sidewise at her and, savagely undulating her head, would utter quick poisonous sounds that trembled with fury. To these the Countess would retort, crooking and undulating, too; thus they would swim with their necks at right angles, raging at each other and crowding for place. Sometimes the Duchess darted her bill out and bit the Countess, who was of a milder nature, I gradually discerned. The admirable ignorance which Sir Francis preserved of all this testified plainly to his moral balance, and filled me with curiosity and respect. Whatever was going on behind him, whether peace or war, he swam quietly on or stopped as it pleased him, with never a change in the urbanity of his eye and carriage.

It came to me that afternoon what his attitude at the woodpile essentially was. He stood there again alone—the ducks were quacking in the pond—and as I looked at his neat white body and the lemon-colored bill and orange-colored legs, all presented in the same dignified profile, I saw that his was by instinct the historical portrait attitude: Perry after Lake Erie, Webster before replying to Hayne. Washington on being notified of his appointment as Commander-in-Chief. And if you smile at my absorption in these little straws from the farmyard you have never known the blessing of true leisure. To drop clean out of my mind for a while the law and investment of trust funds and the self-induced hysterics of Wall Street, and study a perfectly irrelevant, unuseful trifle, such as the family life of Sir Francis and his ladies, brings a pastoral health to the spirit and to the biliary duct.

There was an error in my conclusions about the Countess and Duchess which I did not have a chance to perceive for a day or two, because our domestic harmony was mysteriously disturbed. That clear note in May's voice waked up again, this time a tone or so higher; and it was kept awake by one thing after another. It began after a wagonful of people had passed the ranch on its way down the valley to town. I was off by the river when they stopped a few minutes on the road outside the fence. One could not see who they were at that distance. Jimsy left his ditch work and talked to them and when they had gone returned to it. At our next meal Jimsy's eye was bewildered—and something more— and May's voice was bad for digestion. As soon as my last mouthful was swallowed I sought the solitude of my cabin and read a book until bedtime. How should one connect that wagonload of people with the new and higher tide of unrest? Nothing was more the custom than this stopping of neighbors to chat over the fence, but May's voice and Jimsy's eye kept me as often and as far from their neighborhood as I could get.

It was Scipio, the next time I saw him, who began at once: "Did you see Mrs. Faxon?"

"Who's she?"

"Gracious! I thought everybody in this country knowed her. She's an alfalfa widow."

"Well, I seem to have somehow missed her."

"She went down to town the other day. Pity you've missed her. Awful good-looker."

"Well, I'll try to meet her."

"Her and Jimsy used to meet a whole heap," said Scipio.

"Oh!" said I. "H'm! All the same May's a fool."

"Did she get mad? Did she get mad?" demanded Scipio, vivaciously.

"Lord!" said I, thinking of it. I told Scipio how Jimsy had talked over the fence to the scarlet fragment of his past for perhaps three minutes in the safe presence of a wagonload of witnesses, and how in consequence May had gone up into the air. "To love acceptably needs tact," I moralized; but while I expatiated on this, Scipio's attention wandered.

"You saw Honey Wiggin go up the river with his dudes?"

"Oh, yes."

"And two other parties go up?"

"Yes."

"Any further notions about the game laws?"

"Nothing—except it's the merest charity

to assume they made them when they were
drunk.''

''Sure thing! I guess I'll have a cook when
your camping stuff comes.''

My stuff was due in not many days; and as
I walked home from Scipio's cabin I felt
gratitude to the game laws for the part they
had played in delaying me in this valley
where each day seemed the essence distilled
from the beauty of seven usual days. Even
as I waded Buffalo Horn I stopped to look
up and down the course that it made between
its bordering cottonwoods. A week ago these
had been green; but autumn had come one
night and now here was Buffalo Horn un-
winding its golden miles between the castle
walls of the mountains. Amid all this august
serenity I walked the slower through fear of
having it marred by the voice of May. I lingered outside the house and it was the voice of
the Duchess that I heard. Yes, I was grateful
to the game laws. They, too, caused me to
learn the whole truth about Sir Francis.

On this particular evening I saw where had
been my error regarding the Countess and
Duchess. I have spoken of the Countess'
milder nature, which I thought always put her
behind the Duchess in their struggle for pre-

cedence. It did not. Quite often she made up in skill what she lacked in force and I now saw the first example of it. They were all coming to the pond for their evening swim, the two ducks scolding and walking with their necks at right angles. Sir Francis was in the lead, his head gently inclined toward the water. As he got in the Duchess made an evident miscalculation. She thought he was going to swim to the right, and she splashed hastily in that direction. But he swam to the left. The Countess was there in a flash. She got herself next to him and held her place round and round the pond, crooking her neck and quacking backward at the enraged, defeated Duchess.

. Twice in the following forenoon I saw this recur; and before supper I knew that it was a part of their daily lives. Sometimes it happened on land, sometimes in the water, and always in the same way—a miscalculation as to which way the drake was going to turn. It was the duck who had been nearest to him that always made the miscalculation, and she invariably lost her place by it. Then she would rage in the rear while the other scoffed back at her. Neither of them could have been entirely a lady or they would have known how

to conduct their quarrel without all this dis-
pleasing publicity. But there can be no doubt
that Sir Francis was a perfect gentleman.
Not only was he never aware of what was
happening, but he so bore himself as wholly
to avoid being made ridiculous. That the
Duchess was a little near-sighted I learned
when I took to feeding them with toast
brought from breakfast.

My time was growing short and I began to
fear that I might be gone hunting before I
had penetrated the mystery of the historical
portrait attitude near the woodpile and the
protests of the ducks in the water. This was
going on straight along, only I had never
managed to see the beginning of it. Therefore I fed them on toast to draw closer to
them, and I tried to give each a piece, turn
about; but only too often, when toast meant
for the Duchess had fallen in the water directly under her nose, she would peer helplessly about and the Countess would dip down
quickly and get it. Sometimes the Duchess
saw it one second too late, when their heads
would literally collide, and the Duchess,
under the impression she had got it, would
snap her bill two or three times on nothing,
and then perceive the Countess chewing the

morsel. At this she always savagely bit the Countess; and still, through it all, the drake sustained his admirable ignorance. Finally my feeding device triumphed. I did learn about the woodpile at last.

This is what I saw. They had been swimming for a while after eating the toast. Sir Francis had finally swallowed a last hard bit of crust after repeatedly soaking it in the water. He looked about and evidently decided it was time for the haystack. He got out on the bank, but the ladies did not. He turned and looked at them; they continued swimming. Then he walked slowly away in silence, and as he grew distant their swimming became agitated. Reaching the woodpile, he turned and stood in bland, eminent profile. Then the ducks in the pond began. The Duchess quacked; the Countess quacked; their voices rose and became positively wild. A person who did not know would have hastened to see if they needed assistance. This performance lasted four minutes by my watch—the drake statuesque by the woodpile, the ducks screaming in the water. Then, as I have before described, they succumbed to the power at the woodpile. They swam ashore, flapped to dry themselves, and made for Sir

Francis like people catching a train. He did not move until they had reached him, when all sought the haystack.

So now I understood clearly that it was he who made their plans, timed all their comings and goings, and that they, bitterly as they disliked leaving the water until they were ready, nevertheless had to leave it when he was ready. Of course, if either of them had had any real mind, they would have realized long before that it was of no use to attempt to cope with him and they would have got out quickly when he did, instead of making this scene several times every day. But why did they get out at all when they didn't want to? Why didn't they let him go to the haystack by himself? What was the secret of his power? It was they who were always fighting and biting; his serenity was flawless.

I stood on the breast of the pond, turning this over. If you have outrun me and arrived at the truth, it just shows once again how superior readers are to writers in intelligence. I was not destined to fathom it. Many a problem has taken two to solve it and it was Jimsy who—but let that wait. Jimsy came across from the stable and spoke to me now:—

"What are you studying?"

"I have been studying your ducks."

He looked over at the cabin, where May could be seen moving about in the kitchen, and I saw his face grow suddenly tender. "They're hers," he said softly. "She kind o' wanted ducks round here and so one day I brought 'em to her from town. Then I made this pond for 'em—just dammed the creek across this little gully. Nothing's wrong with 'em?"

"Oh, no. But they've set me guessing."

He did not believe my story, though he listened with his gray eyes fixed on mine. "That's wonderful," he said; "but you've made it up. I'd have noticed a thing like that."

"I don't think you would. You're working all day with your stock and your ditches. Think what a loafer I am."

"It's most too extraordinary," he said, and stood looking at the woodpile. He was not really thinking about what I had told him; I could feel that.

"Well, Jimsy!"

We both started a little. It was May, who had come round the corner of the house, and the setting sun shone upon her and made her quite lovely, where she stood shading her eyes, with a lustrous cloud of hair floating one side of her forehead.

"Well, Jimsy! Dreaming again! Do you know what time it is? The way you've took to dreaming is something terrible!"

Jimsy went into the house.

I was glad that two days more would see me out of this.

Next morning I stood justified—oh, more than justified—in Jimsy's eyes. No one could have anticipated such a performance at the pond as I was able to show him—it bore me out and surpassed anything I had told him—and no one could have foretold that it would fire Jimsy with a curiosity equal to mine.

The ceremony of the toast was in progress when Jimsy, crossing to the corral, saw me thus engaged. He stuck his hands into his pockets and strolled across to the water's edge, wearing a broad grin of indulgence.

"Awful busy, you are!" said he.

"Just watch them," said I.

"Oh, I've got a day's work to do."

"I'm aware," I retorted, "that scientific observation doesn't look like work to the ignorant."

"What're you trying to find out?"

"I told you last night. I can't see how that drake keeps those ducks in order."

"Oh, I guess he don't keep 'em in order."

"I tell you he has them under his thumb."

Jimsy cast a careless eye upon the birds. They had finished the toast and were swimming about. The quacks of the Duchess were merely quacks to him; he did not hear that she was saying to the Countess: "Hah, Hah, Hah! How do you fancy a back seat this morning?"

"One feels mortified, of course," I explained to Jimsy, "that she should betray her spite so crudely—a sad but common thing in our country."

"In the name of God, what are you talking about?" demanded Jimsy.

"Oh, I'm not in the least crazy. New York stinks with people like that."

At this moment the usual thing happened in the pond—the Duchess made a miscalculation. The drake swam suddenly left instead of right, and the Countess jumped to the favored place. Now it was she who quacked backward at her discountenanced rival.

"She is really the sweeter nature of the two," I said. But Jimsy was attending to the ducks with an awakened interest; in fact, he was now caught in the same fascination that had held me for so many days. He took his hands out of his pockets and followed the ducks keenly.

"I believe you weren't lyin' to me," he remarked presently.

"You wait! Just you wait!" I exclaimed.

He watched a little longer. "D'you suppose," he said, "it's his feathers they love so?"

"His feathers?" I repeated.

"Those two curly ones in his tail. They're crooked plumb enticing, like they were saying, 'Come, girls!' "

This reminded me of Jimsy's unbrushed mound of hair and May's coldness at his reference to it. "Feathers would hardly account for everything," I said.

A last spark of doubt flickered in Jimsy. "Are you joshing about this thing?" he asked.

"Just you wait," I said again.

We did not have to wait. In the judgment of the drake it was time for the haystack; the ducks thought it too soon. All began as usual. Sir Francis had reached the woodpile and taken his attitude, the first protesting scream from the pond had risen to the sky, Jimsy's

face was causing me acute pleasure, when the
Duchess did an entirely new thing. She swam
to the inlet and began to waddle slowly up
the trickling stream. Then I perceived a few
yards beyond her the cleanings of some fish
which had been thrown out. It was for these
she was making.

"She has ruined everything!" I lamented.

"Wait!" said Jimsy. He whispered it. His
new faith was completer than mine.

The Duchess heavily proceeded. In my
childhood I used sometimes to see old ladies
walking slowly, shod in soft, wide, heelless
things made of silk or satin—certainly not
of leather, except the soles. The Duchess
trod as if she had these same mid-Victorian
feet and she began gobbling the fish. If this
was any strain upon the drake, he did not
show it. The Countess now discerned from
the pond what the Duchess was doing and she
was instantly riven with contending emotions.
The waves from her legs agitated the whole
pond as she swam wildly; sometimes she
looked at the drake, sometimes at the fish,
and between the looks she quacked as if she
would die. Then she, too, got out and went
toward the fish. I looked apprehensively at
the figure by the woodpile, but it might have

been a painted figure in very truth. I think Jimsy was holding his breath. When a moral conflict becomes visible to the naked eye there is something in it that far outmatches any mere thumping of fists; here was Sir Francis battling for his empire in silence and immobility, with his ladies getting all the fish. And just then the Countess wavered. She saw Sir Francis, white and monumental, thirty yards away; and she saw the Duchess and the fish about three more steps from her nose. She stood still and then she broke down. She turned and fled back to her lord. It cannot be known what the more forcible Duchess would have done but for this. As it was, she looked up and saw the Countess—and immediately went to pieces herself. I had not known that she had it in her to run so.

I cannot repeat Jimsy's first oath as he stared at the triumphant drake leading his family to the haystack. After silence he turned to me. "Wouldn't that kill you?" he said very quietly; and said no more, but began to walk slowly away.

"Now," I called after him, "will you tell me how he manages to keep head of his house like that?"

If Jimsy had any hypothesis to offer then,

he did not offer it, and before he had reached the corral May appeared. I'll not report her talk this time, it was the usual nursery governess affair: did Jimsy know that he had wasted half an hour when he ought to have hitched up and gone for wood up Dead Timber Creek, and didn't he know there was wood for just one day left and it would take him the whole day? I escaped to my fishing before she had done and I took my dinner with Scipio.

At supper I was sorry that Scipio and I had not got off to the mountains that day. Jimsy was still out. He had brought, it appeared, one load of wood from Dead Timber Creek and had gone for another. It was May's opinion that he should have returned by now. I hardly thought so, but this made small difference to May. She was up from table and listening at the open door three times before our restless meal was over. Next she lighted a lantern and hung it out upon a gate-post of one of the outer corrals, that Jimsy might be guided home from afar. In the following thirty minutes she went out twice again to listen and soon after this she sent me out to the lantern to make sure it was burning brightly.

"He would see the windows at any rate," I told her.

But now she had begun to be frightened and could not sit in her chair for more than a few moments at a time.

"What o'clock is it?" she asked me.

It was seven forty-five and I think she fancied it was midnight. If Jimsy had been six years old and a perfect fool to boot she could not have been more distracted that she presently became.

"Why, Mrs. Culloden," I remonstrated, "Jimsy was raised in this valley. He knows his way about."

She did not hear me and now she seized the telephone. Into the ears of one neighbor after another she poured questions up and down the valley. It was idle to remind her that Dead Timber Creek was five miles to the south of us and that the Whitlows, who lived six miles to the north, were not likely to have seen Jimsy. The whole valley quickly learned that he had not come back with his second load of wood by eight o'clock and that she was asking them all if they knew anything about it. In the space of twenty minutes with the telephone she had made him ridiculous throughout the precinct; and then at ten minutes past

eight, while she was ringing up her friend
Mrs. Sedlaw for the second time, in came
Jimsy. The wood and the wagon were safe in
the corral, he was safe in the house and
hungry; and, of course, she hadn't heard him
arrive because of the noise of the telephone.
He had been at the stable for the last ten minutes, attending to the horses.

"And you never had the sense to tell me!"
she cried.

"Tell you what?" He had not taken it in.
"Gosh, but that chicken looks good! What's
that lantern out there for?" He was now
seated and helping himself to the food.

"And that's all you've got to say to me!"
she said. And then the deluge came—not of
tears, but words.

Somewhere inside of Jimsy was an angel,
whatever else he contained. Throughout that
foolish, galling scene made in my presence
before I could escape, never a syllable of what
he must have been feeling came from him, but
only good-natured ejaculations—not many
and rather brief, to be sure. When he learned
the reason for the lantern he laughed aloud.
This set her off and she rushed into the story
of her telephoning. Then, and then alone, it
was on the verge of being too much for him.

He laid down his knife and fork and leaned back for a second, but the angel won. He resumed his meal; only a brick-red sunset of color spread from his collar to his hair—and his eyes were not gray, but black.

That was what I saw after I had got away to my cabin and was in bed: the man's black eyes fixed on his plate and the pretty girl standing by the stove and working off her needless fright in an unbearable harangue.

Audibly I sighed, sighed with audible relief, when the Culloden Ranch lay a mile behind Scipio and me and our packhorses the next day. Jimsy had been as self-controlled in the morning as on the night before—except that no man can control the color of his eyes. The murky storm that hung in Jimsy's eyes was the kind that does not blow over, but breaks. Was May blind to such a sign? At breakfast she told him that the next time he went for wood she would go to see that he got back for supper! I told Scipio that if things were not different when we returned I should move over to his cabin.

"You'd never have figured a girl could get Jimsy buffaloed!" said Scipio.

"He's not buffaloed a little bit," I returned.

"Ain't he goin' to do nothin'?"

"I don't know what he'll do."

Scipio rode for a while, thinking it over. "If I had a wife," he said, "and she got to thinkin' she was my mother, I'd take a dally with her." His meaning was not clear; but he made it so: "I'd take her—well, not *on* my knee, but acrost it."

This I doubted, but said nothing. By and by we were passing the Sedlaw Ranch and Mrs. Sedlaw came running out rather hastily —and began speaking before she reached the gate.

"Oh, howdy-do?" said she; and she stood looking at me.

"Isn't it perfect weather?" said I.

"Yes, indeed. And so you're going hunting?"

"Yes. Want to come?"

"Why, wouldn't that be nice! I thought Jimsy and May might be going with you."

"Oh, they're too busy. Good-by."

She stood looking after me for some time and I saw her walk back to the house quite slowly.

There's no need to tell of our hunting, or of the games of Cœur d'Alène Solo which Scipio and I and the useful cook played at night. In

twenty days the snow drove us out of the
mountains and we came down to human habi-
tations—and to rife rumors. I don't recall
what we heard at the first cabin—or the second or the others—but we heard something
everywhere. The valley was agog over Jimsy
and May. Amid the wealth of details, I shall
never know precisely what did happen. Jimsy
had left her and gone to Alaska. He hadn't
gone to Alaska, but to New York, with Mrs.
Faxon, the alfalfa widow. May had gone to
her mother in Iowa. She hadn't gone to
Iowa; she was under the protection of Mrs.
Sedlaw. Jimsy and the widow were living in
open shame at the ranch. The ranch was shut
up and old man Birdsall had seen Jimsy in
town, driving a companion who wore splendid feathers. There was more, much more,
but the only certainty seemed to be that
Jimsy had broken loose and gone somewhere
—and over this somewhere hovered an epi-
sodic bigamy. But where was Jimsy now?
And May? Had the explosion blown them
asunder forever? Was their marriage lying
in fragments? On our last night in camp we
talked of this more than we played Cœur
d'Alène Solo. If anybody could tell me the
true state of things it would be Mrs. Sedlaw,

and at her door I knocked as I passed the next morning.

"Oh, howdy-do?" said I; and she sat looking at me for some moments.

"What luck?" said she. "Get an elk?"

"Yes," said I. "How are things in general?"

"Elegant," said she. "Give my love to dear May."

"Thank you," said I, not very appropriately.

The lady followed me to my horse. "Seems like only yesterday you came by," was her parting word. She had certainly squared our accounts.

As we drew in sight of the Culloden Ranch you may imagine how I wondered what we should find there. A peaceful smoke rose from the kitchen chimney into the quiet air. Through the window I saw—yes, it was May! —most domestically preparing food. Outside by the pond a figure stood. It was Jimsy. He was feeding the ducks. I swung off my horse and hurried to Jimsy. Sir Francis was eating from his hand.

"How!" said he in cheerful greeting.

"How!" I returned.

"Get an elk?"

"Yes."

"Sheep?"

"Yes."

"Good!"

"You—you're—you're feeding the ducks."

"Sure thing!—Say, I've found .out his game."

I pointed to Sir Francis. "His control, you mean?—how he keeps his hold?"

"Sure thing!" Jimsy pointed to the ducks. "Has 'em competin' for him. Keeps 'em a-guessing. That's his game."

It stunned me for a second. Of course he didn't know that the valley had talked to me.

"Why, how do you do?" cried May, cheerfully, coming out of the house.

Then I took it all in and I broke into scandalous, irredeemable laughter.

A bright flash came into Jimsy's eyes as *he* took it all in—then he also gave way, but he blushed heavily.

"Whatever are you two laughing at?" exclaimed May. She looked radiant. That clear note was all melted from her voice. "Mr. Le Moyne, aren't you going to stay to dinner?"

"Why, thank you!" said Scipio—polite, and embarrassed almost to stuttering.

To Sir Francis Jimsy gave the last piece of

toast. It was a large one. If the drake was aware of the tie between Jimsy's marital methods and his own, he betrayed it as little as he betrayed knowledge of all things which it is best never to notice.

Yes, I am grateful to the game laws. The next legislature made them intelligible.

THE END